PRISON
LIBRARY

D1574959

MAYBE

a Donovan Creed Novel - Volume 9
John Locke

TELEMACHUS PRESS

If you purchased this book without a cover you should be aware that this book is stolen property. It was reported as "unsold and destroyed" to the publisher and neither the author nor the publisher has received any payment for this "stripped book."

This is a work of fiction. All of the characters, names, incidents, organizations, and dialogue in this novel are either the products of the author's imagination or are used fictitiously.

MAYBE

Copyright © 2011, 2013 John Locke All rights reserved, including the right to reproduce this book, or portions thereof, in any form. No part of this text may be reproduced, transmitted, downloaded, decompiled, reverse engineered, or stored in or introduced into any information storage and retrieval system, in any form or by any means, whether electronic or mechanical without the express written permission of the author. The scanning, uploading, and distribution of this book via the Internet or via any other means without the permission of the publisher is illegal and punishable by law. Please purchase only authorized electronic editions, and do not participate in or encourage electronic piracy of copyrighted materials.

The publisher does not have any control over and does not assume any responsibility for author or third-party websites or their content.

Cover designed by: Head of Zeus
http://www.headofzeus.com

Designed by: Telemachus Press, LLC
http://www.telemachuspress.com

Visit the author website:
http://www.donovancreed.com

ISBN: 978-1-937698-82-9

Printed in the United States of America

10 9 8 7 6 5 4 3 2 1

Personal Message from John Locke:

I love writing books! But what I love even more is hearing from readers. If you enjoyed this or any of my other books, it would mean the world to me if you'd send a short email to introduce yourself and say hi. I always personally respond to my readers.

I would also love to put you on my mailing list to receive notifications about future books, updates, and contests.

Please visit my website, http://www.DonovanCreed.com, so I can personally thank you for trying my books.

John Locke

New York Times Best Selling Author

8th Member of the Kindle Million Sales Club
(which includes James Patterson, Stieg Larsson, George R.R. Martin and Lee Child, among others)

John Locke had 4 of the top 10 eBooks on Amazon/Kindle at the same time, including #1 and #2!

...Had 6 of the top 20, and 8 books in the top 43 at the same time!

...Has written 19 books in three years in four separate genres, all best-sellers!

...Has been published in numerous languages by many of the world's most prestigious publishing houses!

Donovan Creed Series:
Lethal People
Lethal Experiment
Saving Rachel
Now & Then
Wish List
A Girl Like You
Vegas Moon
The Love You Crave
Maybe
Callie's Last Dance

Emmett Love Series:
Follow the Stone
Don't Poke the Bear
Emmett & Gentry

Dani Ripper Series:
Call Me
Promise You Won't Tell?

Dr. Gidon Box Series:
Bad Doctor
Box

Other:
Kill Jill

Non-Fiction:
How I Sold 1 Million eBooks in 5 Months!

Acknowledgments

Special thanks to loyal Donovan Creed fan Rick Kocan, a great guy, fellow Penn State fan, and neuroradiologist, who told me about a special MRI machine that could possibly benefit one of the characters in my book. Thanks also to my brother, Ricky, who devoted an entire day of his valuable time to help me make this book that much better, and to Claudia Jackson, of Telemachus Press, who works tirelessly for me, and goes into her "above and beyond" mode almost daily!

MAYBE

Prologue

Miles Gundy.

PRISON
LIBRARY

PEOPLE ARE SCREAMING.

Sunday, last week of May, Derby City Fair, Louisville, Kentucky. Food and people everywhere. Rock bands. Tents. Roaring rides, rumbling roller coasters.

...People are screaming.

Not from rock bands or rides.

People are screaming!

Women's hands. Babies' faces and children's hands are suddenly...melting.

The Derby City Fair is under attack.

But from whom?

And how can the attack be isolated to babies' faces and women and children's hands?

Within minutes, hundreds of cell phones call 911. Hundreds more record the victims and post the videos on YouTube.

The system designed to work swiftly does so. 911 operators contact police, police call the FBI, the Feds call Homeland Security, and by the time Miles "Mayhem" Gundy pulls his late model Honda Accord onto 1-65 South, Homeland Security has Lou Kelly on the phone. Homeland patches the president into the call, along with several members of the Pentagon, who have assembled in the War Room at the White House.

"Where's Darwin?" the president asks.

"We couldn't find him," a man says.

"Who's Lou Kelly?"

"Associate Director, Sensory Resources."

"Mr. Kelly," the president says, "What's happened to Darwin?"

"I have no idea, sir," Lou says. "But I stand ready to help."

"Good man. Mr. Kelly, you're on the phone with Sherm Phillips, Secretary of Defense. Sherm, tell Mr. Kelly what you told me. We need to know what we're up against."

Sherm Phillips does, and Lou tells the president of the United States to hold while he calls Donovan Creed.

Chapter 1

Donovan Creed.

MY DAUGHTER, KIMBERLY Creed, and I are visiting Callie Carpenter at her Las Vegas penthouse. I just told Callie that Kimberly's on the team.

Callie looks amused.

"That seems funny to you?"

She looks at Kimberly. "Mildly so."

I run a group of assassins for a branch of Homeland Security called Sensory Resources. Darwin's my boss. Callie's my top operative. We also do freelance hits for the mob.

Callie says, "When you called from the airport you said Lou Kelly killed Darwin."

"That's Lou's story."

"Seems unlikely," Callie says.

"I agree. But why would he lie?"

"Well, he did try to kill you recently."

"True," I say.

Kimberly's eyes grow wide. "I don't understand. Why would Uncle Lou try to kill you or your boss?"

Lou isn't related to us, but Kimberly's term of endearment shows how close he's become to our family. I don't mind her calling him uncle, though like Callie said, he tried to kill me last year. That incident set our relationship back somewhat, but Lou's a valuable asset, best in the world at what he does, and he's gotten me out of some tight spots over the years. What I'm saying, when he's not trying to kill me, I trust him with my life.

Sounds crazy, right? But that's the type of business I'm in.

I give Kimberly the short answer. "Last year we conducted a sting operation. Large sums of money were involved, and Lou saw a chance to make billions if he could kill me. He couldn't, but I gave him a second chance. To prove his loyalty, Uncle Lou killed Doc Howard, who he claims was my boss, Darwin. He said Darwin was trying to kill me."

Callie says, "What part will Kimberly play on the team?"

"Believe it or not, she's an accomplished assassin."

Callie looks dubious.

"Remember Jimmy T?" I say.

"The one who guarded Kimberly last year?"

I nod. "He quit the business and became a professor at Viceroy College. His real name was Jonah Toth. Kimberly put him down in the men's room."

Callie arches an eyebrow. "I'm impressed."

Most people would ask why Kimberly killed Toth. Not Callie. She could care less why. That's what makes her the world's best assassin, aside from me.

"Including Toth, she's got nine notches on her belt," I say.

"You must be so proud," Callie says, with more than a little sarcasm.

"From now on, we'll call her Maybe. Maybe Taylor."

"I like it," Callie says.

Maybe says, "And I should call you Creed, like everyone else."

"Good point. No sense in broadcasting the fact you're my daughter."

From the kitchen Gwen Peters yells, "You're ignoring me again!"

Gwen is Callie's current love interest. I dated her first, but Callie stole her from me. Kimberly—I mean, Maybe—has met Callie before, but this is her first exposure to Gwen.

"Every time that man enters our house you completely ignore me," Gwen pouts.

Callie smiles and says, "*That man.*"

I smile and say, "*Our house.*"

Callie says, "*That man* is worse than *our house.*"

I agree.

"Hard to imagine how quickly I've sunk so far," I say. "What's she doing in there, anyway?"

"Burning cupcakes."

"Seriously?"

"She's the world's worst cook."

"Maybe I should tell her you said that."

"Maybe I should tell her about Rachel."

My phone buzzes in my pocket. I check the screen.

"It's Lou," I say.

Callie turns to Maybe and says, "Let's go salvage the cupcakes."

As they walk from den to kitchen, I say, "What's up, Lou?"

"Donovan, I've got Homeland Security on the phone, several members of the Pentagon, and the president."

"Hello, Mr. President," I say.

A voice says, "This is Sherm Phillips, Secretary of Defense. The President's monitoring the call, so I'll cut to the chase. We've got word of a bio-terrorist attack at the Derby City Fair in Louisville, Kentucky."

"How can I help?"

"Lou Kelly says you understand terrorists better than anyone in the country."

"I won't argue the point."

"He says you understand how they think. We're blind on this one, and need to know what's happened."

I get a whiff of burnt cupcakes from the kitchen, put my hand over the phone, and yell, "Are you frosting them?"

"We are," Maybe says. "You want one?"

"Chocolate, if you have it," I say.

Back on the phone I ask Sherm, "What do you know for certain about the attack?"

"No bombs detonated, but people's hands and faces have been affected."

"Affected how?"

"The flesh is falling off their bones."

"Can you be more specific?"

"People's hands, babies' faces—appear to be melting."

"How many victims?"

"Somewhere around twenty."

My mind starts racing.

"*Babies?*"

"That's right."

"Their entire face or just the lips and cheeks?"

There's a pause. "Lips and cheeks. How'd you know?"

"You said people's hands. Is it mostly women and children?"

"Yes."

"When you say their flesh is falling off the bone. Which side of their hands is worse, the palms or the back of the hands?"

"Does it matter?"

"What do *you* think?"

"Hold on."

Sherm clicks back on and says, "It's worse on the palms."

"Hand sanitizer," I say.

"Excuse me?"

"Ask if they have plastic hand sanitizing stations at the fair."

"Why?"

"My first guess? This is an urban terrorist, acting alone. He's putting a chemical agent in the public hand sanitizers. Some type of acid. Mom pushes the plunger, foam comes out, she rubs her palms together, then the top of her hands, then pumps some more and rubs it on her baby's hands and cheeks. She can't leave the toddlers out, so she pumps again and wipes their hands. For some reason the acid effect is delayed. But after a time, it starts burning holes in their hands and cheeks."

I hear Sherm in the background. He's on another line, asking if they have hand sanitizing stations at the fair.

Callie, Maybe, and Gwen enter the room. Gwen places a tray of cupcakes on the coffee table. Each lady has her own unique style of attack, but when Gwen licks her frosting the temperature in the room goes up five degrees.

A new voice comes on the line.

"Mr. Creed."

"Yes, Mr. President?"

Callie arches her eyebrows.

"You asked if they had plastic hand sanitizing stations at the fair. Why plastic?"

"Plastic resists acid erosion."

There's another pause. Then the president says, "There are two stations on the midway, two in the exhibit buildings. All four have plastic reservoirs. I think you've done us a great service."

"Thank you sir."

He says, "It terrifies me to know there are people like you in the world."

"Rest easy, Mr. President. I'm on your team."

"That's what frightens me."

I say, "You understand this is just the beginning?"

"What do you mean?"

"You need to get the word out to all airports, public buildings, private businesses, anyone who uses plastic dispensers in bathrooms or work spaces. Especially Louisville, and the surrounding cities and towns."

"You're joking."

"Not remotely."

"You said it's one man, acting alone."

"That's what makes him so dangerous."

"We need to catch him."

"Good luck with that."

He pauses. "Could you catch such a man?"

"If he continues attacking? Yes. But it'll take time."

"How much time?"

"If he stays busy? Days or weeks."

"Then catch him."

"I'll need the full cooperation and resources of government and law enforcement."

"Excuse me?"

"I'll need the highest possible clearance."

"You're joking."

"Total access, Mr. President. Nothing less."

He says, "I wouldn't give a man like you access to a dog turd."

"Thank you, Mr. President."

The line goes dead.

Maybe says, "You were talking to the president just now?"

"Yes."

"Of the United States?"

Gwen makes a face and says, "Bullshit. He was just trying to impress me. He'll say or do anything to get in my pants."

She looks at me and says, "It won't work."

Her tongue flicks at the frosting again and again, and I see she's making little sculptures on her cupcake. Callie catches me staring.

"Down boy," she says.

Chapter 2

LOU CALLS ME back.

"Good call on the hand sanitizer," he says.

"Any deaths yet?"

"No. But they're going to be permanently disfigured."

"That bothers me."

"Me too. Wait. Which part?"

"The acid should start burning mom's hands immediately. But there's a delayed reaction of what, ten, maybe fifteen minutes? Possibly longer?"

"You're trying to guess how long it would take him to put acid in all four sanitizing stations?"

"I am. Ask the Louisville PD how far apart the stations are, from first to fourth."

"Will do."

"And ask the geeks how he managed to delay the effect."

Lou's geek squad possesses the finest computer minds and researchers on the planet. It's one of the reasons I keep him on my personal payroll.

"I'll run it by them," he says. "Anything else?"

"I want to know every victim's name. I want to see their before and after photos."

"Even the babies?"

"Especially the babies."

"This will help you find him, somehow?"

"No. But it'll help me *want* to. And Lou?"

"Yeah?"

"When the scientists isolate the chemical agent, we need to learn who manufactures it, who distributes it, and how our urban terrorist got hold of it."

"What type of person are we looking for?"

"A chemist."

"Corporate?"

"Yes. Or a high school chemistry teacher, college professor, or grad student with a chemistry major."

"That's a pretty wide range."

"First cut."

"What do you mean?"

"Everyone with a chemistry background has survived the first cut. As Felix continues terrorizing people, we'll narrow the possibilities accordingly."

"Felix?"

"We need to call him something besides the urban terrorist."

I hang up and tell Callie and Maybe about Felix and what he's done.

"Sounds like a kid's book," Maybe says. "*Felix at the Fair?*"

Callie says, "I thought we were going to war against Darwin."

"We are. If he's alive."

"Then what's all this about finding Felix?"

"We're a long way from finding Felix. But it'll keep Lou busy while I try to figure out if Darwin's still alive.

Chapter 3

Sam Case.

THE GOVERNMENT FACILITY at Mount Weather, near Bluemont, Virginia, includes an underground bunker called Area B, which is the size of a small city. Area B was built to withstand repeated strikes from nuclear weapons. More than 600,000 square feet in size, Area B contains a hospital, crematorium, dining and recreational facilities, self-contained power plants, and is equipped to broadcast TV and radio signals.

Area B is where Sam Case lives and works for the government, developing a synthetic cure for the Spanish Flu, a virus so deadly it decimated one-third of the earth's population in 1918. The thing about the Spanish Flu, there's no cure. First time around, it nearly wiped out the planet.

Next time it'll be worse.

And there will be a next time.

Like many government employees, Sam's in no hurry to solve the problem he's been hired to solve. But Sam's motivation isn't about steady employment. It's about self-preservation. Sam's life is in jeopardy, and Mount Weather is the only place on earth his enemies can't get to him.

What you want to know about Sam Case, he's one of the world's most brilliant people. More than a year ago he had a thriving business and a hot wife, Rachel. His business involved moving billions of dollars electronically from bank to bank, all over the world, twenty-four hours a day, effectively hiding it for the world's most ruthless dictators and criminals. The modest fees he charged earned him millions of dollars, and life was good.

Enter Donovan Creed.

Creed also parked a sum of money with Sam, but unlike the others, he saw an opportunity to cash in. He broke into Sam's house, lived secretly in his attic, and eventually breached Sam's security and stole billions of dollars from Sam's clients.

He also stole Sam's wife, Rachel, who's certifiably insane.

She's also one of only two people in the world known to possess a gene that's resistant to the Spanish Flu.

Rachel also lives in the underground bunker in Area B.

But not by choice.

Government scientists are holding her captive, harvesting her eggs, and hoping to create a generation of children who will inherit the gene. Until Sam or some other scientist can create a synthetic response to the Spanish Flu, Rachel must remain there.

Sam considers Donovan Creed his arch enemy. Such is his hatred for Creed, he'd give ten years of his life to make Creed suffer a day.

Sam measures his life in terms of victories he's won over Creed.

His first was separating Creed and Rachel. He orchestrated Rachel's capture, and manipulated scientists into letting him live and work in Area B so he could be near her. Sam's sperm is being used to create the new children from Rachel's eggs. Having sole access to Rachel, and being the man responsible for creating children with her, Sam hoped, over time, to win back his wife's affection.

Not that he wants the bitch. He only wants to sleep with her. And only because it would be another way to punish Creed.

Pretty sad when the victory you hope to claim over your arch enemy involves sleeping with your own wife.

But Rachel has no interest in sleeping with Sam, so that part—that one small part—is another victory for Creed.

Worse, Creed doesn't seem overly broken up over the fact his girlfriend is stuck in Area B for what could be years.

Sam's second victory involves Creed's daughter, Kimberly. Sam's been fucking her.

What makes it particularly sweet, he's manipulating her into loving him.

And Creed, the deadliest assassin on earth, hasn't a clue.

The man who made this revenge possible is another of Creed's enemies, Doc Howard. For all practical purposes, Kimberly is Sam's car, and Doc Howard gave him the keys to her ignition.

Doc Howard expects to be compensated.

For starters, he demanded that Sam locate the Bin Laden death photos. These, like many of the world's most sensitive documents, are stored in the underground vault at Area B.

Sam has no idea what Doc Howard plans to do with the photos, but it's best to stay on Doc's good side. He's a very dangerous and powerful man in his own right.

Sam used his hacking skills to locate and copy the digital files.

He's looking at them now, with mild interest. When he's finished looking, he encrypts the photos, and types a code to bypass computer security for twelve seconds while he forwards them to Doc Howard's email account.

Doc gets some stupid photos, Sam gets Kimberly Creed.

He presses a button on his cell phone.

Kimberly answers, using her alias.

"Maybe Taylor."

Chapter 4

Maybe Taylor (Kimberly Creed).

"HI MAYBE," SAM says. "How's tricks?"

"I can't talk now," she whispers. "I'm with my father."

"In Vegas?"

She works her way out of the den, onto Callie's balcony. "Okay, I can talk now. Yeah, I'm in Vegas."

"I miss you," Sam says.

Maybe smiles. "That's ridiculous. It's only been a day."

"Seems like forever."

She likes being the one with power in the relationship. It lets her be cool, lets her say things like, "Don't fall in love, Sam."

Which forces him to say, "Sorry. Too late."

"Are you still planning to divorce your wife," she says, "or was that something you said to get in my pants?"

"We're definitely divorcing. The papers are being drawn up this week. She's already agreed to sign them."

"Don't do it hoping to marry me," she says.

"Why not?"

"We're never going to be a couple."

He changes the subject. "I've found a guy to do your boob job."

She laughs. "I hope it's a doctor and not just some guy."

"Don't worry. Your boobs will soon be in the hands of a highly-skilled surgeon."

"Odd way to put it," she says.

"It seems insane to pay another man to put his hands on your body. He should pay you for the privilege."

"Hmm. Maybe I should charge you next time!"

"If that's what you want, I'll gladly pay."

"Assuming there's a next time," she says, then smiles, noting his silence. Maybe loves being able to manipulate him for a change. For the past year he's been a demanding, judgmental father figure. Now, after one night in the sack, she's turned him into a lovesick puppy. Sam spent a year scrambling his voice, manipulating her over the telephone, and all that time he thought he was in charge. Now he's met her, had sex, and his power has crashed and burned. He's fallen head over heels for her, and she loves it.

He says, "There has to be a next time."

Maybe can hardly contain her joy. In truth, she expected he'd probably never call after getting what he wanted. That's happened more than once with boys in the past, so she assumed a grown man would be even more aloof.

Especially a married man like Sam.

But as it turns out, she has the power to make him happy or sad. It's an amazing feeling, one she's never experienced.

Sam says, "I have to have you again."

"Why?"

"Excuse me?"

"What's the big deal?"

He sighs.

She loves it when he sighs. He's frustrated, working hard to win her affection.

"You're the best I ever had," he says.

"The best what?"

"Lover."

She smiles and says, "That can't be true."

"I'd take a lie detector test on it."

"You're older, wealthy, and married. This is all about you getting a little strange on the side. You probably fucked me, thinking of your wife."

"That's not true, Kimberly."

"Wrong name, Sam."

"Sorry."

"You expect me to believe I'm the best you ever had?"

"Absolutely."

"Have you forgotten my sexual issues? You had to inject my vagina with Botox to get it open. I felt nothing. It can't have been a pleasant experience for you."

"It's not just the act, it's the whole experience. It's being with you, holding you, touching you. Helping you achieve sexual comfort. I know it sounds absurd, but I've never felt this way in my life. If you don't like me calling it love, I'll call it passion, though it's love, passion, and a hundred other things combined. I'm not trying to push you, honey. But I have to have you. And yes, you're the best I ever had."

"The best what?"

"I already told you."

"Say it again. Be vulgar."

"The best fuck."

"Say it again, with feeling."

"You're the best fuck I ever had!"

"Thanks, Sam."

She feels something warm and exciting stirring within her...

And likes it.

"When can I see you again?" he says.

"I'm not sure. I'm working for him."

"Who, your father?"

"Yes."

"Have you told him about me?"

"He still thinks you're a post-Rapture pet salesman."

"Have you told him my real name?"

"He asked, but I refused. We're still calling you Chuck."

"If he demands to know my name, what will you say?"

"I'll tell him to fuck off."

"He's your boss now," Sam says.

"I freelance. I work for him, I work for you. If someone else comes along, who knows?"

"Prove it."

"Prove what?"

"That you work for me."

"How?"

"Kill him."

"Who, my father?"

"Yes."

She laughs. "I'd kill you before raising my voice at him."

"I know. I was just kidding. But I think I've made my point. You obviously don't work for me."

"I'm not sure you understand what free-lance means, Sam. It means I get to accept a contract if I want it."

"But if you work for me..."

"As I said, I work for both of you. But he comes first."

Maybe smiles, knowing he's pouting. Sam's got it bad for her. It'd be so easy to take advantage of the situation.

She says, "Give me another way to prove my loyalty."

"Kill someone for me."

"Who?"

"I don't care. As long as it's someone your father knows."

"He knows Doc Howard."

Maybe notes the complete absence of sound on the other end of the line.

Finally, Sam says, "Did you say Doc Howard?"

"Yes."

"You think you can kill him?"

"He's already dead."

"What?"

"One of my father's people killed him. I just heard about it. Apparently he was far more than a skilled surgeon. He was one of the most powerful people in government. My father called him Darwin. He was my father's boss."

More silence.

And still more.

Finally Sam says, "Kill someone else your father knows. I want details."

Maybe removes the phone from her ear and stares at it a moment while frowning. Is he serious? She puts the phone back to her ear.

"You seem to have forgotten the financial component," she says.

"It's all about the money to you."

"That's right."

"Pleasing me means nothing to you?"

"Don't pout, Sam. It's a turn off."

He sighs again. Then says, "Fine. Pick out a victim. Someone your father knows. Tell me who it is, and the connection, and I'll formulate a price."

Creed, Callie, and Gwen are sitting in the den, talking. Maybe watches them through the sliding glass door, and allows her gaze to settle on Callie. Creed certainly knows Callie. But Callie's as deadly as Creed. And anyway, she likes Callie. She's beautiful, smart, and cool, everything Maybe wants to be. Callie's not a candidate for killing. There's still too much to learn from her.

Gwen, on the other hand...

She looks at Creed, looking at Gwen.

Maybe's not jealous of Gwen, doesn't mind Creed looking at women that way. She wants her father to be happy, and bedding sexy women seems to make him quite happy.

If he's happy, she's happy.

She's also not jealous that Gwen's prettier and sexier than she is, and has great hair and a better body.

What she doesn't like about Gwen is her disrespect.

20

Callie and Creed deserve to be respected. They're elite killers. Gwen's a twenty-year-old widow and former stripper. She's got no right to disrespect Callie or Creed.

And yet she disrespected both of them.

Earlier, in the kitchen, Gwen made a nasty remark about how Creed tricked her into having sex with him. Callie's eyes narrowed, and Maybe could tell it was a sore subject, though Gwen hardly seemed to notice or care.

Gwen cheated on Callie with Creed.

On the phone, Sam says, "You still there?"

"Yeah. Wait a sec."

Maybe watches Gwen working it for them, licking the frosting off her fingers and lips like a porn star might do.

She's center stage, full of herself.

Thinks she's hot shit.

It's disgusting.

Maybe didn't notice it before, but Gwen's wearing a particularly revealing outfit. Creed noticed. He's noticing it now.

You know who's a better match for Callie? she thinks to herself.

Creed!

Callie's prettier than Gwen, and tougher, and she and Creed are in the same business. They work together, respect each other. Callie's sexy, but doesn't throw it all over the place like Gwen. With Gwen out of the way, Creed and Callie might find happiness, despite Callie's apparent preference for women.

Maybe imagines holding a gun on Gwen, forcing her to her hands and knees.

Bark like a dog! she'll say, and Gwen will bark.

Louder, bitch! and Gwen will howl.

Kiss my feet! she'll say, and sexy, hot-shit Gwen will kiss Maybe's feet.

"I've got someone in mind," Maybe says.

"Who?"

"Gwen Peters."

"Never heard of her."

Maybe stares at her phone again, in disbelief.

"Why would you know her?"

"I wouldn't. Who is she?"

"My father's girlfriend."

"You're sure about that?"

"Why wouldn't I be?"

"No reason. I'm just surprised to hear he has a girlfriend."

"Why?"

"I don't know. Forget I said it. Are they currently dating?"

"My father had sex with her a couple of times."

"When?"

"What do you care?"

"Humor me. I'm trying to come up with a price."

"I don't know the first time. Second time was a few days ago. She's Callie's girlfriend."

Maybe notes a distinct pause on the other end of the line.

Then Sam says, "Who's Callie?"

"She works on our team."

"Callie's an assassin?"

"Yup."

"Your father fucked Callie's girlfriend?"

"Yup."

"I bet that caused problems."

"I suppose."

"Tell me."

"I don't know much about it. And anyway, what do you care?"

"How old is Gwen?"

"Twenty."

"Just like you."

"So?"

"Is she pretty?"

"I suppose."

"Are you jealous of Gwen?"

"Of course not!"

"You're okay with it? Her having sex with your father?"

"Why wouldn't I be? Oh, wait. I see. You think I want to fuck daddy. That's ridiculous to the point you're about to piss me off. That whole thing about how you made me call you Daddy last year? I told you before, it's creepy as hell. And disgusting. You're lucky I ever let you touch me, and I probably won't, ever again."

"Sorry. You're right, of course. Still, you'd like to see Gwen suffer, wouldn't you?"

Maybe can tell Sam's trying to get in her head. She knows how to deal with him.

"Tell you what. I'll pick someone else."

"No!"

Maybe smiles.

Sam says, "I'll pay you a hundred grand to terminate Gwen. But I want details."

"She's close to Callie and my father. You'll have to provide the weapon. Something foolproof. If Callie finds out, I'm toast."

Sam goes quiet a minute. Then says, "I've got something in mind. When can we meet?"

"You'll come to Vegas?"

"I can be there tomorrow night."

"Let me know when you get here."

PRISON
LIBRARY

Chapter 5

Sam Case.

SAM CAN'T BELIEVE his good fortune!

Having your enemy's daughter kill your enemy's girlfriend? That'd be a hell of a victory for anyone in the revenge business.

Of course, Sam's not just anyone.

He's a genius of the highest order. The type of genius who can parlay this type of news into something really special. He presses a button on his cell phone.

Rachel answers.

"Hi honey," Sam says. "Got a minute? I need to talk to you."

"Is this about our divorce?"

"It's about Kevin."

When Creed seduced Sam's wife, Rachel, he told her his name was Kevin. She liked it, and sticks with it.

"Kevin calls me every week," Rachel says. "But he won't say where he is or what he's doing."

"Let me visit and I'll tell you what I know."

"When can you get here?"

Sometimes Rachel forgets they live in an underground bunker. Separated by halls and walls, not states or countries.

"Thirty seconds," he says.

"Make it five minutes. I need to get dressed. Wait, is it something bad? He's not dead, is he?"

"No."

"Good. I love him."

"I know."

Sam hangs up and tries Doc Howard's phone number. Maybe says Doc Howard has been killed. If that's the case, Sam might be off the hook. He might not have to steal any more classified information from the government. He wishes he hadn't sent the Bin Laden photos. If someone gets into Doc's computer, they might be able to trace the photos back to Sam.

Someone answers the phone.

"Hello, Sam."

The voice on the other end is electronic, and sounds exactly the same as Doc Howard.

"Doc?"

"Doc Howard is dead. Of course, you've already heard this news."

"Who is this?"

"Listen carefully, Sam. Are you listening?

"Yes, sir."

"Your deal with Doc Howard, aka Darwin, is hereby cancelled."

Sam pauses, perplexed. He tries to work it out in his mind, but there's insufficient data.

"I don't understand," he says.

"You're done."

"Are you...you're not planning to kill me, are you?"

"No. But we can no longer protect you."

"What do you mean?"

"You stole billions of dollars from some really nasty people."

"I didn't steal it. Donovan Creed did."

"Maybe you can explain that when they come to call."

"We can still work together."

"In what possible capacity?"

"Did you receive my recent email?" Sam says.

"You're testing me?"

"It seems appropriate, under the circumstances."

"If you're referring to the Bin Laden photos, I destroyed them, along with everything else on Darwin's computers. You're off the hook Sam."

"You seem to know everything Doc Howard knew. I think you're him."

"I could care less what you think. You called me, remember?"

"I called Doc Howard."

The man laughs. "It doesn't matter who you call, Sam. I'm always listening."

Sam says, "Doc Howard might be dead, but you're Darwin."

The man says nothing. Is Sam right? Could this be the real Darwin? And if so, does it matter?

Sam says, "What about Kimberly Creed?"

"You might want to re-think having Kimberly kill Gwen Peters."

"How can you possibly monitor my cell phone calls?"

"Child's play, Sam. Why do you want her to kill Gwen?"

"When Creed finds out his daughter killed his girlfriend, he'll hit the ceiling. It's part of the sweet revenge Doc Howard and I spoke about."

Darwin clucks, as if chiding a young boy. "Use your head, Sam."

"What do you mean?"

"There's a much better hit out there for you."

"Which hit is that?"

"Sherry Cherry."

"Who?"

"Your mother-in-law."

"Well, this time you're wrong. My mother-in-law is Sherry Birdsong."

"She's using her maiden name these days."

"Sherry Cherry?"

"That's right."

"You're joking! And even if you're not, why would I want to kill Rachel's mother? She's a junkie."

"Creed brought her to Sensory Resources, placed her under Doc Howard's care. As soon as she's clean, he plans to exchange her for Rachel."

"What?"

"Sherry and Rachel have the same gene. Creed worked a deal with the government to exchange them, after Sherry gets clean. And we're talking days, Sam, not weeks or months. Now that Doc Howard's dead, Creed will find someone else to certify her as clean. If that happens, you'll spend years of your life in the hole with your mother-in-law instead of your wife."

Sam slaps his hand against his head. Idiot! How could he fail to consider the possibility Sherry might have the same gene as her daughter?

"Does Rachel know about the exchange?"

"No. She only knows Creed promised to get her out. But that's his plan."

"If I kill Sherry, Rachel has to stay underground until we develop a cure for the Spanish Flu."

"That's right. And from what I understand, you're what, ten years away?"

"At least."

Darwin says, "You want to really beat Creed? Have his daughter kill Rachel's mother. You'll have Rachel and her future children all to yourself for at least ten years."

"If Sherry's at Sensory Resources, Kimberly can't touch her."

"Correct. But now that Doc Howard's dead, I'll see to it Sherry gets released. I can coordinate it to fit your schedule."

"You'll see to it?"

"That's right. I suppose that makes you think I'm Darwin? Fine. Call me Darwin."

How would it work?"

"When Sherry gets released she'll need a ride to the airport." I'll have the driver take her to a location that's suitable for killing."

"This might be the best day of my life!" Sam says.

"Glad I could be a part of it," Darwin says.

Sam's joy doesn't last long. He feels his ears burning. He grits his teeth. It's a proven fact Sam's a genius of the highest order. Ten times smarter than Creed! So how is it Creed always manages to stay a step ahead of him? Darwin has done him a huge favor, revealing Creed's plans.

But at what cost?

Sam says, "What do I owe you for this information?"

"Nothing. This business about Rachel's mother is for my own amusement."

"This whole scenario about the shared gene never crossed my mind. I don't understand how Creed got it and I didn't."

"It was too obvious, Sam. Creed's an undisciplined thinker."

"He thinks outside the box?"

"No. People who think outside the box start with the box. Creed doesn't even know there's a box."

Sam says, "Of course there's a box. It's a metaphor for all you know about a specific situation. Using that as a starting point—"

"Don't beat yourself up about it," Darwin interrupts. "This thing between you and Creed amuses me. On paper, it's all you. But Creed's got your number."

"Why is that, do you think?"

"It comes down to logic, and critical thinking."

"No one in the world is more logical than me!" Sam says, indignantly. "Compared to me, Spock the Vulcan is Porky Pig!"

"That's your weakness, Sam. Your facility for logical, deductive reasoning makes you as predictable as the days of the week. Your arch enemy Creed is the most undisciplined, illogical, irrational opponent you could possibly face. He's everything you aren't, starting with insane."

"He doesn't play fair," Sam says.

"That reduces it to the lowest common denominator," Darwin agrees.

"You've saved me a decade of misery," Sam says.

"Assuming you make the kill."

"I'll make it. Then I'll destroy Donovan Creed."

"No you won't. But I like your attitude."

Sam says, "You know Creed better than you know me, but don't sell me short. The smart money bets on Creed, I get that. So my chances of beating him are less than fifty percent. But what's a realistic assessment? Thirty, thirty-five percent?"

"Statistically?"

"Yes."

"I could be wrong. I don't want to discourage you."

"That's okay. I want your honest opinion."

"Zero."

"That's ridiculous."

"Sam, you need to put things in perspective."

"I'm listening."

"Compared to your brain power, Creed is as insignificant as an ant."

"That sounds about right," Sam says.

"Except that you're an angry little boy, and Creed is all the ants in the world."

"What the hell's that supposed to mean?"

"Assume you're standing in your yard, and an ant bites your ankle. It burns. You get angry and stomp on the ant hole and crush it. After a time the ants dig their way out and one of them bites you again. Furious, you grab your garden hose and flood the colony. A few days later, you're in your kitchen, drinking coffee, when an ant bites your foot. You run outside and pour gasoline down the ant hole and light it. In the process, you set your clothes on fire and get burned half to death. While you're recuperating in the hospital, the ants continue building their colony. By the time you get home, you're weaker than you started, but the ants are twice as strong."

"With all due respect Darwin, what's your point?"

"When the ants bite you, it's not personal. It's what they do."

"That's it?"

"In part."

"What's the rest?"

"At the end of the day, you're nothing but an angry little boy."

"And what's Creed?"

"A force of nature."

"Fuck Creed!"

"That's the spirit, Sam."

Chapter 6

Rachel Case.

SAM LOOKS HAPPY, sitting in the chair by the wall.

Rachel's sitting on the side of her bed, facing him in a room so small their knees are practically touching.

"Where's Kevin?"

"Las Vegas."

"Why?"

"I'm not sure."

"How long's he been there?"

"At least a month, off and on."

She lets that information roll around in her head until she loses track of it.

She says, "Kevin's my boyfriend."

Sam nods. "Have you ever heard the name Gwen Peters?"

"I don't think so. Why?"

"She's an unusually pretty, platinum blonde."

"How old?"

"Twenty, I think, and a former stripper. She was married to a gambler named Lucky Peters."

Rachel moves her mouth to one side and nibbles at the corner of her mouth.

"A stripper? Why would I know a stripper?"

Sam says, "I hate to be the bearer of bad news, but she's been fucking Kevin."

Rachel leaps to her feet and slaps him with her right hand. As he tries to cover up, she makes a fist with her left, and connects with his jaw. She rears back to slap him again with her right hand, but he grabs her wrist, then—shit!—takes another left hook to the face. He can't time the left while holding the right, so he ducks under her arms while standing, and lifts her off her feet and throws her backwards, onto the bed. As she tries to sit up he pins her arms, but leaves his face exposed. She head-butts him, connecting with his nose.

Sam feels it break.

He howls and jumps back and runs out of the room to the infirmary.

Kevin is only allowed to call Rachel once a week, on Sundays, but Rachel can call him anytime, if she gets permission from Major Jordan's office in Area B. She calls the major's office, a secretary logs her in and dials the number. Kevin often ignores her calls, but this morning, to Rachel's surprise, he answers.

"Hi baby!" Kevin says.

"You're in Las Vegas?"

"I am. How'd you know?"

"Who's Gwen Peters?"

"You remember Callie Carpenter?" he says.

"The blonde."

"Right. Anyway, Gwen is Callie's girlfriend."

"That's not what I heard."

"What did you hear?"

"You've been fucking her."

"Who told you that?"

"Doesn't matter. I'm going to kill her!"

"You're in an underground bunker," Kevin says.

"But I'm getting out soon, you said so yourself. And when I do, I'm going to slice her throat and stab her eyes. Then we'll see how pretty she is! Then I'm going to follow you around and kill everyone you look at! Then we'll go to bed and make love. When you fall asleep, I'll stab you eight million times!"

"How's that psychiatric treatment going for you?" he says.

"You think that's funny? You think I like being stuck here in this shit hole? You think—"

A strange noise comes over the line. Kevin's voice is breaking up. She can't understand him, but it doesn't matter. Rachel's got something to say, and says it ten times before hanging up.

What she says is, "Gwen Peters is gonna die!"

Chapter 7

Miles Gundy (Felix).

WITH THE DERBY City Fair attack behind him, Miles knows the police will keep a close eye on plastic containers. That will last what, three weeks? In two months they'll let their guard down, and if Miles is still alive, he'll nail a public office building's restroom. People are used to liquid soap. They won't give it up without a fight.

State fair officials around the country will stop using hand sanitizers. Government offices might need a little extra coaxing.

Miles catches his reflection in the interior mirror of his Honda Accord and says, "You know what this means? It means you made a difference, Miles! You changed the system."

He smiles.

It's a beautiful Sunday afternoon in central Tennessee, and everything's going his way. He created mayhem in one state, today will make two. Miles slides a CD into the slot on the dashboard and jerks his body to the maniacal beat of his favorite tune, Demon Devil Dog, as it thunders from six speakers of surround sound. His Accord offers 160 watts of total stereo output, and Miles is leaving no watt unused.

At this decibel level, one tune's enough. When the song's last shriek dies down, Miles glances at the mirror and says, "From now on every man, woman, and child will have to stop and think before washing their hands in a public place. Something they took for granted their whole life will now be a source of fear."

He nods at himself and adds, "Thanks to you."

He cruises the tony neighborhood of Blair, a suburb of Nashville, till he sees what he's looking for.

Balloons and a poster.

Balloons and a poster lets the whole world know a kid is having a birthday party. All you have to do is follow the arrow on the signs. Miles shakes his head in disbelief, thinking how the unsuspecting parents are leading him to the killing field. After today, no parent will dare put up balloons and a poster to direct guests to their children's birthday parties.

State by state, event by event, Miles will change the way people live their lives.

What better way for a dying, unemployed chemist to achieve immortality?

Miles follows the posters to the party location, turns into the long driveway, parks by the other cars in the circle. He pops the trunk, removes a giant, double-stuffed cookie cake, and carries it to the front door.

He balances the giant cake in his left hand, while pressing the door bell with his right.

A bored teenager opens the door and directs him through the house to the backyard. As the children recognize the brightly-colored box, they rush to surround Miles. Two of the moms clear off a space on the poolside table to accommodate the cookie cake.

Miles's eyes follow the movements of one of the moms, a pretty redhead, who looks up in time to catch him staring down her blouse. She gives him a disgusted look that shows what she thinks of a delivery man who's crass enough to attempt a down-blouse while surrounded by children at a kids' birthday party.

Miles smiles broadly and says, "Happy Birthday!" then leaves. No one thinks to ask if there's a bill to pay. No one offers him a tip, or escorts him back through the house. As he stands in the kitchen, looking around, he considers sneaking through the house. He probably has time to do some truly dastardly things.

But why push his luck?

He works his way to the foyer, opens the front door, gets in his car, and backs out the driveway.

Miles purchased the pre-made cookie cake in a busy mall in Indianapolis two days ago. It'll be slightly stale, but the kids won't notice. They also won't notice the miniscule amount of ricin poison Miles dusted over the top of the filling. It was a bitch getting the top layer of cookie off the cake and back on again, and it didn't turn out quite as pretty as it was when purchased, but again, the kids won't care.

Miles hopes the pretty redhead mom with the pale pink bra samples the cookie cake.

Chapter 8

Donovan Creed.

I'VE ONLY BEEN in Vegas a few weeks, but I've already made an investment. I purchased a plastic surgery center and day spa I plan to open when the police release the building to me. They're still investigating a mass murder that took place on the premises. I'll start fresh with a whole new staff headed by Dr. Eamon Petrovsky, the world's greatest plastic surgeon. Dr. Petrovsky (I call him Dr. P.) headed the team of surgeons that gave me the new face I'm wearing.

Earlier today I called Dr. P. and told him to pack some clothes for our trip.

"What trip?" he said.

"We're flying to Louisville, Kentucky."

"Why?"

"What do you care? Until our license is granted, you're unemployed."

I told him I'd swing by his place at three and give him a ride to the private airfield. Then I went for a run, worked out in Callie's gym a half hour, then took a shower. After packing an overnight bag, I found the women glued to the TV in the den.

"What's happened?" I ask.

"Remember Mindy Renee Whittaker?" Callie says.

I think a minute. "The kid who got kidnapped years ago?" Callie nods.

"What about her?"

"She's been in witness relo. But someone just blew her cover!"

"What kind of asshole would do that?"

"They're not saying. But ten to one it's her husband."

"She's married? How's that possible? She's just a kid."

"Time flies. Believe it or not, she's twenty-four now."

I scoot onto the couch next to Maybe and watch the drama unfold. It's so weird, calling my daughter Maybe, but it's something I need to get used to.

The photo they're showing of Dani Ripper's a good one, designed to build ratings.

She's hot.

Chapter 9

"WHY ARE WE flying to Louisville?" Dr. P. asks.

We're at his place. I'm carrying his luggage.

"Where's your medical bag?"

"You didn't mention bringing it."

"I shouldn't have to! You're a doctor! What if I get shot or something?"

"Relax, Donovan. It's only a matter of retrieving it from the den."

He leaves to fetch it.

An hour later we're airborne, thanks to Bob Koltech, who owns and operates a fleet of six jets. Bob and I have a great relationship. In return for giving me instant service and personally flying me wherever I wish to go, no questions asked, I pay Bob twice his normal fees.

Dr. P. says, "Did you hear they found Mindy Renee?"

"She's Dani Ripper now. It's all over the news."

Indeed, it's a compelling story. Even Callie's hooked. One network promised around-the-clock coverage as the story develops, so Callie and the others are having a Dani party tonight, complete with pizza and cheese bread! Such fare is no big deal for me, but these ladies are extremely calorie conscious.

At ten forty-five local time we land at General Aviation, near Standiford Field in Louisville. Bob has a limo waiting for us, and within twenty minutes Dr. P. and I are strolling through the lobby of the Seelbach Hotel.

We check in, grab a drink together, and go to our respective rooms. While getting comfortable I turn on the TV to catch the latest on Dani Ripper.

Like Callie said, Mindy Renee Whittaker's all grown up now. At twenty-four, she's blossomed into one of the prettiest women I've ever seen, assuming the photos are authentic. They say she's a private investigator, working out of Cincinnati. Changed her name to Dani Ripper nine years ago.

Dani Ripper? As in Jack the Ripper? Odd name for a girl to make up.

But I like it.

And I like her.

I find myself wondering if a gorgeous private eye like Dani Ripper might be interested in working with me. I fire up my laptop to see what the internet says about her.

More photos.

Stunning. Not as sexy as Gwen, but prettier.

Not as beautiful as Callie, but close.

And there's this: she's married.

That's her husband on TV, holding a press conference in front of their house.

Ben Davis. But Dani goes by Ripper, not Davis. I wonder why.

I also wonder why Dani's not with Ben at the press conference. Then I think about it and decide she's probably inside, hiding. Ben says she's staying at a friend's house, but that's probably untrue.

If she is staying with a friend, that's a hell of a lucky friend!

I listen a few minutes, and...wait. Is he actually trying to pitch a book deal? I wonder if maybe Dani and her husband wrote a book and then leaked the story themselves.

Clever.

I like the fact she's married. Means she likes men.

I catch myself, and laugh.

What is it about men? Why do we always visualize ourselves dating or sleeping with the woman we're thinking about at any given minute?

I laugh again, forced to admit that's what I was thinking just now. About how Dani, like Callie, is breathtakingly beautiful, and how I'd give anything to have sex with Callie, but Callie prefers women, which takes me out of the game. And I was thinking how Dani Ripper's as close to Callie as a man is likely to find on this earth, and that led me to think, well, Dani's married, so she likes men, which means I have a chance!

I might be more insane than Rachel.

But now that I'm all worked up, a powerful urge comes over me. There are two or three women I could call to satisfy that urge, and one is local. But for some reason I can't explain, only one woman will do on this particular night.

Miranda Rodriguez.

Miranda's a grad student at NYU, working toward her master's in counseling psychology. Smart, witty, pretty, she's the whole package.

"Donovan!" she squeals. "I was just thinking about you!"

"Still angry I canceled the Chicago trip yesterday?"

She laughs. "Don't be silly! That wasn't your fault. Your daughter surprised you with a visit. That's a wonderful thing!"

"True. So why were you thinking about me just now?"

She laughs again, harder.

I love Miranda's laugh. Can't describe it except to say it reminds me of the tinkling of piano keys and a waterfall.

I know, I know.

"Spill it, Miranda. You won't hurt my feelings."

"Well...I've got a tuition payment coming up."

Right. So of course she was thinking about me. You see, Miranda's fucking her way through college. Tuition and living expenses being what they are in NYC, it's either earn the money or take out a school loan for three hundred grand.

"When can we get together?" I say.

"Name it, handsome," she says, and I feel her warmth coming through the phone.

"Tonight?" I say, knowing she'll say it's too late.

"Can you arrange a private jet?"

"I can."

"Seriously?"

"Seriously!"

"Omigod!" She squeals. "I'm so excited!"

I look at my watch.

Eleven twenty-two.

If Bob Koltech picks her up, we'll lose three hours. One for him and the co-pilot to drive to the airport and get the jet ready, and two to fly to Teterboro Airport. Then two hours back, and another thirty minutes before Miranda can get to my hotel.

5:00 a.m.? That won't work. I'll have Lou Kelly book a private jet from NYC.

"I'll have a limo at your place in fifteen minutes," I say. "By the time you get to Teterboro, the jet will be ready to roll. "You can be here in three hours."

"How many days?"

"Pack light."

"Oh, Pooh."

"If you stay longer we can shop for whatever clothes you might need."

"That's my boy!" she says.

"Can't wait to see you," I say.

"Me too!"

We're both quiet a minute. Then she says, "It's not just about the money, Donovan."

"I know."

"I really like you."

"I know that, too."

"I just don't want you to think...you know."

"I do know."

"I mean, nobody treats me like you."

"Miranda?"

"Yes, sweetheart?"

"Pack your shit."

"Okay."

She makes a kissing sound and we hang up. Then I call Lou and have him make the arrangements. He doesn't ask if I'm in Louisville, and I don't volunteer the information.

With that done, I call room service and order a bottle of their finest bourbon, two tumblers and flutes, and champagne on ice for Miranda. I'd wait a couple of hours on the champagne, but room service shuts down at midnight.

When the guy brings my order, I ask where the ice machine is, knowing I'll need to refill the bucket in a couple of hours. As he leaves, Lou calls me back to say Miranda's on her way to the airport.

He says, "Have you seen the news?"

"Dani Ripper?"

"Hell of a story!" Lou says. "Can't wait to read the book."

"I'd read it just to hear what went through her mind when she learned about the door key."

"No kidding! You think she broke the story to sell the book?"

"Probably. And if it's money she's after, she'll be flush with clients soon enough."

"I'd hire her just to look at her," he says.

We both go quiet, allowing our thoughts of Dani Ripper to go where they may.

Breaking the mood, I ask, "Anything new on Felix?"

"No. But I'll have all the victim information by tomorrow."

"Thanks, Lou."

Chapter 10

Miranda Rodriguez.

MIRANDA DOESN'T LIKE the way the limo driver keeps looking into his mirror, staring at her. It's nearly midnight, the road shiny, slick with rain. It wouldn't do to have an accident. She presses the button on the armrest and holds it while the glass between her and the driver goes up. She continues holding the button until the thick material of the divider rises to block his view completely. She doesn't want to be rude, but he seems to know what she's up to, and he's made her uncomfortable.

She takes this opportunity to call her new best friend, who says, "Miranda! Hi!"

"Did I wake you?"

"No, of course not! I'm a night owl. What's up?"

"I'm meeting Donovan Creed tonight."

"Yes."

"You...knew?"

She laughs. "How could I possibly know?"

"You don't sound surprised."

"It was my first thought why you might call me this late."

"He's flying me to Louisville on a private jet."

"And you're excited."

"Yes."

Her friend's voice is warm. "You like him," she says.

"I do, Rose. A lot."

"That's good. I'm so happy you do." Rose pauses, then adds, "It's late. Are you tired?"

"I'll sleep on the jet."

The two friends are quiet for a moment.

Miranda says, "I'm excited and scared at the same time."

"Enjoy the feeling. And remember everything we talked about."

"I will. And thank you so much for everything!"

"It's an exciting time for both of us," Rose says.

Three hours later, Miranda knocks on Creed's hotel room door.

Chapter 11

Donovan Creed.

MIRANDA LOOKS LIKE a million bucks. By the time I shut the door behind us, she's on me like fire on a match head! Between kisses it dawns on me the polite thing to do is offer her champagne, but then I realize propriety—like Miranda's clothing—has been left at the door.

"Do me!" she says.

I smile. "Right now?"

"Do me!"

"No drinks or chitchat?"

"Do me!"

I do her.

Then roll onto my back to catch my breath.

After a few minutes Miranda says, "Are you comfortable?"

"And then some."

She sits up in bed, flashing a sly smile.

"I hope you're not too tired," she says.

"Because?"

"Because sex is like pancakes."

"Pancakes," I say.

"Uh huh."

"Do tell!"

"When you make pancakes, you always toss out the first one."

"Ah. And that's because?"

"The purpose of the first pancake is to get the skillet warmed up just right."

"In this example, which of us is the skillet?"

"That would be me," she says.

"And this means?"

"I'm going to rock your world!"

"Right now?"

"If we haven't used up all the batter."

I sit up, figuring we'll start with a kiss. But she pushes me back gently and says, "I'll take it from here, Flapjack!"

"Okay."

There are two absolutes where hookers are concerned.

One, cash is king.

Two, you get what you pay for.

The escort food chain ranges from street walker to courtesan. Top of the list initials include C, PS, and GF, in that order, and less than one percent attain it.

GF stands for girl friend experience. Young ladies fresh in the business naively offer clients a girl friend experience, a claim that triples their hourly price. But it's usually unsustainable. Before meeting the first client it seems plausible a young lady could fake a warm smile, be super friendly, and tongue kiss Richard Gere from Pretty Woman, and—oh yeah, have romantic sex with him.

But the guy who shows up to claim her kisses looks nothing like Richard Gere. In fact, he probably looks a lot like the very men she finds disgusting, and would never look at, much less kiss. That first hour will prove to be the longest of her life. Her client will go to the internet boards and post he had a rip off experience. After a few negative reviews the young lady will no longer be able to charge GF prices.

Those who truly offer a GF experience are few and far between, and they earn every penny they get.

PS means porn star. Women who promise their clients a Porn Star experience should be prepared to make a serious physical commitment. Clients who pay a premium for PS aren't looking for missionary.

C stands for courtesans, the rarest of the elite. Courtesans represent the highest form of professional romance. You don't just call a phone number and request a courtesan. You meet her in a neutral setting, exchange conversation, and she makes the decision to date. You want a relationship with a true courtesan? You'll have to pass an interview, and give references for two prior GF's. And yes, she'll interview your references!

Courtesans are guaranteed to be beautiful, intelligent, charming, witty, fun, sensual, and classy. These are the women who turn heads at formal parties and keep conversations flowing. They're also great listeners, highly empathetic, and have a thorough understanding of the three or four men they're willing to date.

And they're expensive.

A good courtesan can earn thirty grand a week.

Miranda's a very good courtesan, my all-time favorite, and she's put a glow on me I haven't felt in a long time. If you know me, you know I live a high stress lifestyle. These sessions with Miranda let me unwind and completely relax. A few hours later, I'm ready to take on the world.

I'm lying next to her now, listening to her sleep. I kiss her shoulder and wish she weren't so brilliant. If she were less intelligent it would take her much longer to get her degree, and I'd have more time to be with her.

See, she intends to stop hooking after graduating.

Wait.

I didn't think to ask if it bothers you I pay for sex.

Does it?

I know professional sex is frowned upon by a high percentage of the population. But there are worse vices, believe me. And I can make a strong argument all sex is bought, sold, bartered, or stolen.

But I'll save that discussion for the second bourbon.

In the meantime, I'll leave you with this thought. There are three options for consensual sex, and two of them involve affairs. In other words, you can be married or single, and you can fuck someone who's married or single...

And that's it.

Single on single, married on married, or married on single.

Within those options, you can pay for sex or get it free.

With so few choices available, I try not to judge people. What works for you is fine with me, provided you don't step on my toes. Yes, I pay Miranda for sex. But she and I are both single, and love spending time together. And when we do, no one gets hurt.

Which is worse, single people paying for sex or married people having an affair?

Argue among yourselves. It's late, and I've got an early morning.

Chapter 12

IT'S UNSEASONABLY WARM at 8:00 a.m. in downtown Louisville, and destined to get hotter. By 2:00 p.m. the heat index is expected to hit a buck-twelve, thanks to the legendary Ohio Valley humidity. But no matter. Dr. P. and I will be in Virginia by then. Miranda, too.

Miranda's a real trooper.

After learning why Dr. P. and I came here, she asked to join us. I tempted her with sleeping in and ordering room service, and warned it wouldn't be pleasant. But she insisted, and that's why we're enjoying a cup of coffee in the hotel restaurant, waiting on Dr. P.'s phone call. He's across the street, at Jefferson Memorial Hospital, arranging clearance for us.

Miranda sips her coffee and smiles. Yes, she's paid to smile and be pleasant on three hours' sleep. But most women in her situation would've been happy to stay in bed and order room service.

At a separate table a few feet away, a young brunette in business attire is staring holes in us over a bowl of oatmeal. Miranda seems not to notice, or care. This is one of the many things I love about being with her in public. Miranda's half my age, but not the least self-conscious about our relationship.

She says, "You're beautiful!"

I laugh. "That's my line for you."

"It applies, though."

I shrug. "Sounds silly when you say it. I mean, I'm old enough to be your father."

She shakes her head. "Donovan?"

"Yeah?"

"Accept the compliment."

"Okay."

"Asshole."

I check to see if she's smiling.

She is.

The young brunette at the table next to us has removed her cell phone from her purse. I think she's texting about us to one of her girlfriends.

"This is something I need to work on?" I ask. "Accepting compliments?"

"It is. But we've discussed this several times."

"I know."

"I won't be here much longer," she says.

"I know."

She gets to her feet and leans across the table to give me a kiss. The local businessmen at the table behind her enjoy the view her short skirt offers, while the brunette beside us looks to be retching, as if she swallowed some bad seafood.

Miranda kisses me a second time and says, "You're going to miss me, aren't you?"

I kiss her back, and sigh. "I will. But what I'll really miss?"

"Tell me."

"Us."

She sits down, reaches across the small table, and takes my hand. "I'll miss us too."

She sees the look in my eyes and says, "Don't ask."

"Too late."

"If you don't ask, I won't cry," she says.

"I already asked. With my heart."

The intrusive brunette rolls her eyes, props her cell phone on the table and snaps a picture of me with one hand while pretending to signal a waiter with the other. Then she adjusts the angle and takes a picture of Miranda.

She's annoying the shit out of me, as are the businessmen sitting behind Miranda. When one of them says to his friends, "Kiss him again, honey," and the others giggle, I think about the popping sound their eyes will make if I burst them with my fingers. I always thought that sound was caused by a little pocket of gas behind the cornea, but according to Lou's research, the eyes contain no such gas, and the popping sound has more to do with the clear jelly of the vitreous body needing a place to escape in a hurry.

Speaking of eyes, Miranda's are gorgeous, and she has impossibly long, natural eyelashes models would kill to possess. She uses them to blink a couple of tears from her eyes.

"I'll say it again, Donovan. We can't keep seeing each other after I graduate."

"Maybe not like last night," I say. "But when you get your license, I'll be your first client."

"You can't. It wouldn't be ethical."

"You've been counseling me for a year."

"Not professionally. I can't counsel a client with whom I've been intimate."

I frown. "That's a stupid rule. Who could possibly understand me better, a total stranger, or a woman who knows me intimately?"

She smiles. "You're not going to draw me into a debate on this issue."

"Why not?"

"First, you're too persuasive. And second, you're right. But this license is very important to me. I've worked very hard to earn it. In order to keep it I have to follow certain rules of conduct."

"These rules are important to you?"

She gives me her analyst look, the one she uses when trying to give the impression she's speaking to me as an equal. Since I already know she's smarter than me, her look doesn't have the intended effect. It only makes her more adorable in my eyes.

She says, "You're trying to suck me in again."

"You think?"

"If I say I believe in following rules of ethical conduct, you'll remind me I'm already breaking them by sleeping with you for cash. Which I'll attempt to justify by saying it was a means to obtain the finest education. But then you'll say I could've gotten a school loan, and I'll say if I got a school loan I never would have met you."

"All of which is true," I say.

"Yes, but then you'll point out we did meet, and—"

"Miranda?"

"Yes, honey?"

"Exactly how long do I have?"

She bites her lip.

"Miranda?"

She blinks more tears from her eyes.

The lady at the table next to us is hanging on our every word. I noticed her jaw drop a moment ago when Miranda said she'd been sleeping with me for cash. Now she's glaring at us in a rude fashion.

Miranda notices too, because she turns to the brunette and says, "Excuse me, have you ever considered whoring?"

"I beg your pardon?"

"Would you consider a three-way? You, me, and my boyfriend?"

"Excuse me?" The young brunette's face is beet red. She looks at me with total disgust.

I blow her a kiss. She does a double-take, and intensifies her glare.

Miranda says, "We've got a room upstairs. We can bang one out in ten minutes if you're in a hurry to get to work."

"What? You can't possibly think I'd—Are you insane?"

Miranda says, "I hope you don't expect us to believe you got that round mouth by eating oatmeal."

"Omigod!" she says, and jumps to her feet to run tell the manager.

"I guess that's a no," Miranda says. "Sorry, Donovan."

"Story of my life," I say.

My cell phone vibrates. I answer it.

"Yes?"

"We're good to go," Dr. P. says.

Chapter 13

DR. P. MEETS us in the lobby and escorts us to Dr. Boreland's office. Boreland is Chief Operating Officer of Jeff Memorial.

Dr. Boreland shakes my hand while looking at Miranda. "And you are?"

"Miranda Rodriguez," she says, extending a hand.

He says, "You're quite young. How do you fit in?"

"I'm sixteen weeks away from obtaining my Master's in Counseling Psychology. After graduating, I'll work with Dr. Petrovsky at his clinic, counseling patients."

He nods.

Dr. P. is stunned into silence, which reminds me I neglected to tell him Miranda's cover story.

Dr. Boreland shows us close up photos of the victims and says, "Dr. Petrovsky claims he can do something with these hands and faces. Do you share his optimism?"

I look at Dr. P.

He nods.

I say, "Dr. Petrovsky is the most highly-skilled surgeon on the planet Earth."

Dr. Boreland frowns. "You'll pardon me for doubting the veracity of that claim."

"Whoa," I say. "You couldn't have said that simpler?"

He frowns.

I say, "I can assure you Dr. P. is without peer."

"Funny I've never heard of him."

"Have you heard of Albert Schweitzer?"

"Yes."

"Sigmund Freud?"

"Yes."

"Phineas Flatulence?"

"Do I strike you as the sort of person who enjoys having his time wasted with childish humor?"

"Why do you ask?"

Dr. Boreland decides to move on, saying, "Dr. Petrovsky's name fails to appear in any internet listing of doctors and surgeons."

"And yet you're showing us the photos," I say.

He shows me a flat, annoyed smile. "I've been ordered to cooperate fully."

"By?"

"Dr. Dame, president and Chief Executive Officer."

"That should convince you."

"It convinces me Dr. Petrovsky has a great deal of clout. But I strongly disapprove of him giving false hope to these patients."

I look at Dr. P. "Show him the photo."

Dr. P. opens his leather folio and removes two photographs of an incredibly handsome man who happens to have a prominent scar on his face.

Dr. Boreland studies the photos a full minute, then looks at me.

"So?"

"That's me, less than four years ago."

"That's preposterous."

I notice Miranda's eyes are glued to the photos. She might be more stunned than Dr. Boreland. I exaggerated about being incredibly handsome just now. I was, at best, good looking. Now, thanks to Dr. P. and his team of government surgeons, I'm incredibly handsome.

For real.

Dr. Boreland opens his desk drawer and removes a pair of surgical magnifying loupes. He puts them on and walks around his desk.

"Do you mind?" he says.

"Not at all."

He motions me to look up so the light catches my face. Then he leans over until our faces are less than a foot apart. He pinches my face in various places, holds the skin between his fingers, and inspects it.

"This is a joke," he says.

"Thank you," Dr. P. says.

Moments later the three of us exit Dr. Boreland's office and take the elevator to the fourth floor.

All twenty-two Derby City Fair victims were brought to Jeff Memorial. The thirteen adults, six children and three infants were doubled up and grouped in adjoining rooms on the fourth floor so they could be treated and monitored consistently.

I approach the first woman, Mary Valentine.

"Hi Mary, I'm Donovan Creed. This is Miranda Rodriguez and Dr. Eamon Petrovsky."

Mary is drugged to the max. Her hands are heavily bandaged, and she's receiving fluids.

She tries to speak, but her words are slurred.

Miranda says, "We'll check on her and let you know."

I have no idea what that means. Miranda says, "She asked about her daughter."

Dr. P. and I exchange a look that indicates he didn't catch Mary's question any better than I did.

I continue, "Dr. Petrovsky is the world's greatest plastic surgeon. He believes he can significantly restore your hands, over time. Dr. P. and I own a surgery center and spa in Las Vegas, Nevada. When you're able to travel, we'd like to donate our services to you and your daughter, free of charge."

Mary's eyes well up. She mumbles something completely incoherent. Dr. P. and I look at Miranda, who says, "Mary is very grateful, but wants to know how long it will take."

Dr. P. says, "Best case, five years, twenty surgeries."

Mary mumbles something else. Miranda translates, "What about her baby?"

Dr. P. says, "Don't expect a miracle."

More mumbling. Miranda says, "She wants to know if it will hurt."

"It will be excruciating," Dr. P. says. "I'm sorry, I wish I had better news."

Mary would never imagine the total cost of her surgical procedures, medicine, physical and occupational therapy will cost more than three million dollars. Nor would she care, I suspect. Right now she's in a state of shock. Her attack was so sudden, her situation so horrific. One moment she's pushing her baby in a stroller at the fair, the next moment her hands are burned practically to the bone. Not to mention her baby's beautiful face has been ruined forever.

All this happened because she decided to use the free hand sanitizer dispenser at the fair.

As we go from one patient to the next, Dr. P. offers hope, Miranda offers encouragement, and I offer revenge.

Whoever did this is going to pay.

Chapter 14

Maybe Taylor.

"WHAT DO YOU mean she broke your nose?"

"She smashed my face with her head."

"How did she manage to get that close to you?"

"I was trying to hold her down on the bed. She became hysterical and started thrashing about. Wait. That didn't translate properly."

"No shit it didn't! So what's the bottom line, no divorce?"

"The divorce is a certainty. She was upset about something else."

Maybe knows Sam sucks when it comes to explaining situations where he's completely innocent. She decides to move the conversation along.

"Are you coming to Vegas or not?"

"My plane lands at two-forty."

"I'll call you at three to see where you're staying."

"I've booked a suite at the Vega Rouge. Just come when you can, call me from the lobby."

"You feel up to making the trip?"

"No. But I feel up to seeing you."

Chapter 15

Donovan Creed.

AFTER LEAVING THE hospital Miranda and I cross the street and enter the hotel quietly. I feel her staring at me.

"Are you okay?" she says.

"I'm good."

She nods.

We walk down the hall in silence, enter the room, sit on the bed.

She says, "Can we talk about this?"

"Are you sure it's ethical?" I say, and immediately wish I hadn't.

She ignores my comment and says, "I know you, Donovan."

She thinks she knows me. In truth, she knows very little about me.

"This has affected you deeply."

She's right about that.

"Look at me," she says.

I know what she's going to say. She's going to tell me I need to clear my head of evil thoughts. She'll say that giving total strangers more than fifty million dollars worth of free treatment is stunningly generous, and I should reflect on how their lives will be improved because of me. She'll tell me not to dwell on the bad. She'll say I need to forgive the person who did these terrible things, and move on with my life.

But when she speaks she says none of those things.

What she says is, "You're going to catch the bastard that did this. And when you do, you're going to torture him in the cruelest possible way."

"Yes."

Then she says, "You won't turn him over to the authorities. You'll make sure he's dead."

"Yes."

"But I need to be there, Donovan. I need to talk to him."

I look at her. "Why?"

"I need to understand his thought process. I need to know what makes him tick."

"It'll make you a better psychologist?"

"I believe it will."

"Do you want to participate in the torture?"

"No. But I want to watch."

We stare at each other a moment.

Then we attack.

To put it more accurately, Miranda attacks me. She slaps my face with both hands as hard as she can, over and over, stopping only to fall on her back and rip her blouse open.

I take this as a cue to remove the rest of her clothing, which is no easy task while getting the shit slapped out of me.

Now, entering her, I expect the slapping to stop. But it intensifies! Again and again she slaps my face. She eventually makes her hands into fists and flails away at my face. Miranda's not a skilled fighter, so I lean into her punches to intensify the effect.

When she bloodies my nose and lips she gets excited and starts bucking me. I ride it out as long as I can, which roughly translates to eighty seconds.

As you might imagine, this type of fucking is exhausting, hard work.

When we finish we're panting like overweight dogs after a two-mile sprint.

Miranda says, "Are you okay?"

"I am."

"Good. Now it's my turn."

I look at her. "What do you mean?"

"I'll get on top while you hit me."

Chapter 16

I DIDN'T HIT Miranda.

But she did manage to talk me into pulling her hair from behind.

A little.

After a hot shower I inspect my puffy face and split lip in the bathroom mirror while thinking about Miranda's perfect ACT score and her lifetime four-point-oh grade point average, and wonder briefly about the direction modern psychology is taking.

We pack everything except her torn blouse, and meet Dr. P. in the lobby, where I notice him staring at the scratches on my face.

"It took three years to create that face," he says. "Show some respect, will you?"

"Sorry, Doc," I say, while winking at Miranda.

Two hours later our pilot, Bob Koltech, expertly guides his jet onto the private runway outside Roanoke, Virginia, and taxies as close to the private aviation building as he can get. I sign the form, grab the rental car keys, and drive Miranda and Dr. P. to a hotel on I-81 just north of 581. Miranda and I check into our room, brush our teeth, and meet in the restaurant for sandwiches.

Dr. P. says, "I'm not sure why I'm here."

"I've got an errand to run."

Miranda says, "Can I come?"

"Yes."

I look at Dr. P. "How about you?"

"I hate that place," he says. "If it's all the same to you, I'll stay here and read."

"What place?" Miranda says.

"Sensory Resources," Dr. P. says. "Headquarters."

Miranda says, "Does this have anything to do with the acid guy?"

"We're calling him Felix," I say. "And no, it doesn't."

"Why Felix?"

I shrug.

Dr. P. says, "Do you have any objection to me catching a commercial flight back to Vegas?"

"I might need you."

"Why?"

"I don't know. It's a feeling I have."

"A feeling."

"That's right."

He frowns again. "Fine."

"You can sit in the sun by the pool."

He puts his index finger in the air and spins it around. "Whoopee!" he says.

"I thought old people loved sitting in the sun, by the pool."

"Fuck you," he says.

Chapter 17

"AM I ALLOWED to be pissed off?" Lou Kelly says.

Miranda and I are in the rental car, headed south on 81, bound for Sensory Resources, in Bedford, Virginia.

Wait. I know what you're thinking. Bedford's east of Roanoke, not south.

You're right. I mean, that's what I've always told you.

But it's not true.

I'm trusting you with this because...well, because I trust you. You've known me awhile, now, and you deserve the truth. Sensory isn't near Bedford. It's eighty miles south-west.

Why did I lie?

We've always lied about the actual location. It's what I programmed my staff and all the workers to say.

Here's why:

Bedford's a small town, where everyone knows everything about everyone else. There are people in Bedford who contact us when strangers show up asking questions about Sensory Resources, Donovan Creed, Lou Kelly, Callie Carpenter, Jarvis Kent, Jeff Tuck, Joe Penny, and the various assassins and bomb-builders who work for us, as well as the doctors and security personnel who work at the Sensory facility.

Those who come to Bedford seeking information...stay in Bedford, if you get my drift.

Lou doesn't know we're forty minutes away from paying him a surprise visit, but he's on the phone and pissed because he just learned...well, I'll let him say it:

"I busted my ass to get you the victim photos, then I hear you spent the morning viewing not only the photos but the victims themselves!"

"Relax, Lou."

"This is why you had me fly Miranda Rodriguez to Louisville last night? You could've saved me hours of work by telling me your plans. It's not like I'm sitting around, twiddling my thumbs all day."

"Listen. Twiddling your thumbs all day is hard work. Don't let anyone tell you it's not."

"Hilarious. Look, if you want to catch Felix, we can't do the same things. You're wasting my talents and resources."

"I agree. This was a spur-of-the moment decision. I hoped to interview the victims, see if they saw anyone suspicious."

"Did they?"

"Yes. They saw Felix. And Santa, Elvis, and the Tooth Fairy. They were so drugged up they could barely think."

"I could've told you that before you made the trip."

"I know. But I wanted to see them for myself, in person. It fuels me."

I put Lou's call on speaker. Then ask, "Any news on Felix?"

"If I had anything, I would've called you."

"I believe you. But where would we be if I failed to ask?"

"It's been less than two days since the fair. You expect him to do something this soon?"

"Yes. This is an angry corporate chemist. Probably lost his job recently, so he's got free time, fresh supplies, and a whole lot of pent up aggression. If we let him cool off or run out of supplies, he'll probably quit."

"That's a good thing."

"If he quits, he gets away with it."

"True. But the world's a better place."

Miranda and I exchange frowns. I say, "So he cools off, gets another job, and gets fired again. What then?"

Lou says, "What made you narrow him down to a corporate chemist? Why can't it be a high school or college professor?"

"Did you see the photos of the kids' faces?"

"Yes."

"You think a teacher would do something like that?"

"A crazy one, maybe."

"This is an angry corporate chemist. He's been fired recently."

"Not retired?"

"No. Retirement is something you see coming. Felix is angrier than that. He's been fired for doing something wrong, or because of the economy. Get your geeks to search that angle."

"Will do."

"Keep me posted."

"I will. By the way, the CFO at Jefferson Memorial said you're paying the victims' expenses."

"After they leave the hospital."

"That's a helluva generous offer. But what if Felix does this five or six more times before we catch him?"

"I'll go broke."

We hang up and Miranda says, "You know that much about Felix already?"

I frown. "Truth is I know nothing about Felix. I'm just following my gut."

"You're certain he purposely targeted kids and moms?"

"I am. Why?"

"Assuming you're right, you may want to add something to his profile."

"What's that?"

"He's recently divorced, or legally separated. He's lost his wife and kids to the legal system."

I look at her and smile. "How about you forget about private practice and come to work for me?"

She laughs. "That'd be a hoot."

"I'll make it worth your while."

"How so?"

"A hundred grand a year?"

"To work for you? No way!"

"Name your price."

She laughs again. "I'll think about it."

"No you won't."

"No, I won't," she agrees.

"Will you marry me?"

She smiles. "You're a nut."

"I notice you didn't say no."

Before she can, I get Lou on the phone again. When he answers I say, "My fiancé and I have been talking."

"Fiancé? You mean Miranda?"

"Yes. And she gave me a clue."

"Guess that's better than clap."

I pause, and Lou says, "Sorry. That was uncalled for. I thought you were joking."

"About the clue?"

"About her being your fiancé."

"I was. But the clue is sound."

I tell him to have his geeks search for a recently divorced father who either works or recently worked as a chemist.

"This is really good, Donovan," Lou says, excitedly. "It's highly searchable."

"Don't thank me," I say. "Thank my fiancé. You're on speaker."

"Aw shit," he says. "I'm really sorry for the remark, Ms. Rodriguez."

"No harm done," Miranda says. "But Lou?"

"Yes?"

"If I'm not overstepping my bounds, I think your researchers should also look for any crimes against women and children."

"A woman or child is attacked every second."

"I'm talking about groups of women or children. Like a teacher and her entire class. Or a day care. Or a church or camp outing."

"You okay with this, Donovan?"

"Absolutely. In fact, I like Miranda's profile better than mine. I still think we've got an angry corporate chemist, but maybe he's not recently fired. Maybe he's recently divorced or separated."

"I'll type it all in and see what spits out."

"Good man."

A half hour later Miranda and I enter Sensory Resources and walk down the corridor to my office. I punch in my key code to unlock the door, open it, and see Lou Kelly fucking Rachel's mom, Sherry Cherry. He's got her bent over my desk, taking her from behind.

Chapter 18

LOU TURNS TOWARD us, his face red from the effort. He gasps, closes his eyes, shakes his head, mortified.

Sherry hasn't seen us yet, but notices her lover has stopped in mid-thrust.

"Everything okay back there, hon?" she says. "You're not done, are you?"

I say, "If Felix is in there, you've probably subdued him by now. Step away, and we'll help you drag him out."

Sherry jumps, causing Lou to slip out of her. He deftly pulls his pants up and says, "I wish I had something clever to say."

Sherry pushes herself to a standing position and yells, "What the fuck are you doing here?"

"I could ask you the same, since it's my office. By the way, I think you owe my desk an apology."

She looks like one of those "What's Wrong with this Picture?" photos, standing as she is with her hair and makeup freshly done, wearing diamond-studded earrings and an exquisite matching necklace, a beautiful silk print blouse, but naked from the waist down. She spins around and tries to walk across the room to fetch her skirt from the chair against the far wall, but her panties are bunched around her ankles. Lou, ever the gentleman, drops to a knee and tries to slide them up her legs as she's doing the penguin walk. His interference causes her to trip. She falls to the floor and cries out, but Lou won't be denied. He keeps tugging her panties up her legs. When he gets them to her thighs, she slaps his face and hoists them up the rest of the way. Then gets to her feet, puts on her skirt, smoothes it down with her hands, and says, "Who's the bimbo?"

To Miranda I say, "I've told you about my girlfriend, Rachel?"

She says, "Yes, of course. Is this her?"

I laugh. "No, this is Rachel's mother."

"You think this is funny?" Sherry says. "We'll see how funny it is when I tell Rachel you're fucking this one."

"My name's Miranda."

"I don't give a shit! You could be Martha fucking Washington, for all I care! What I want to know is what are you doing with my daughter's boyfriend?"

Miranda looks at me.

I look at Sherry.

"How've you been, Sherry? You appear sober."

"You're not putting me away, Donovan. You want to make someone miserable? Let Miranda spend some time in that nasty fuck hole."

Miranda says, "No thanks. I saw the view from both angles just now, and it's not working for me."

I say, "Sherry's talking about the underground bunker at Mount Weather. That's where Rachel's eggs are being harvested by government scientists."

Miranda says, "See? This is why I love hanging out with you! Where else am I going to hear these types of conversations?"

I look at Lou. "You told Sherry about Mount Weather?"

"I did," Lou says.

"But how did you know about the exchange?"

"Doc Howard told me."

Sherry says, "I don't give a rat's ass who told who!"

"Whom," Miranda says.

"Fuck you, whore!" Sherry says. She turns to me and says, "You're not exchanging me for Rachel. Tell him, Lou."

"Yeah, tell me, Lou."

Lou clears his throat and says, "I agreed to let Sherry leave. We've got no right to hold her here against her will."

"I agree."

"You do?"

"Yes. But I'll take her."

Sherry looks at Lou. "Kill him if you have to, Lou. But don't let him touch me!"

Lou gives me a pleading look, and I can see what's going on. Lou's been romancing Sherry, telling her how important and powerful he is. To gain her confidence, he told her my plans to get her sober and exchange her for Rachel. Then he promised to protect her from the big, bad Creed. Bought her expensive jewelry and clothes, and eventually seduced her. But now I've popped in, and Lou's afraid Sherry's going to see him in a different light.

"Let's talk about this outside," Lou says.

"Fair enough."

He and I step outside. As we do, my phone vibrates. It's Sal Bonadello, crime boss.

"What's up?" I say.

"My Fourth of July party," he says.

"You already invited me."

"What about your blonde? You said you'd ask her. What's her name? Callie? My party needs—whatcha call—pizzazz! Callie in a bikini? Yowzer!"

"Callie's not a party animal."

"Talk her into it."

"I don't know, Sal. The kind of people you'll have there…"

"What about them?"

"Someone's bound to hit on her."

"So?"

"Callie hits back."

"What's that mean?"

"She might kill some of your guests."

"I'll put the word out. Hands off this one. But I gotta see her. And you."

"You want me to wear a bikini too?"

"No, jerk wad. I might have some—whatcha call—gainful employment for you."

"We'll see."

"We'll see, we'll see. That's all you ever say."

I hang up and look at Lou.

"Have you even bothered to tell your geeks to start searching the parameters we gave you?"

"Of course." He looks at his watch. "They've been on it about forty minutes now."

"This thing with Sherry Cherry," I say. "How long has it been going on?"

"Long enough. I love her, Donovan."

"She's been here less than two months."

"Doesn't matter. Things are good between us."

"Are you saying we're at an impasse?"

He stares into my eyes, searching for hope. Finding none, he says, "Can you at least give us a few days?"

"Give me proof Doc Howard is Darwin, and that he's dead."

"If I provide it, you'll let her stay?"

Yesterday Rachel threatened to kill Gwen. I believe her, she's killed before.

"I'm in no rush to have Rachel on the outside," I say. "She's getting worse. If you can protect Sherry, she can stay here until I'm convinced Rachel's functional."

"I told Sherry she could leave."

"She leaves with me or stays here on the compound. Those are your choices."

"Why?"

"If something happens to Sherry, the government will never release Rachel."

"Maybe they shouldn't."

"Maybe not. But I hope you don't intend to take that option away from me."

"Me? Of course not! I love Sherry. I want her here."

"You're aware of her history with drugs?"

"Yes."

"You'll protect her?"

"Yes, absolutely."

"I have your word?"

He pauses, knowing what that means.

"Yes," Lou says. "You have my word."

We go back in the room. Sherry looks at Lou, hopefully.

I say, "Sherry, there's good news and bad. Which do you want to hear first?"

Chapter 19

Sam Case.

THE TRIP TO Vegas is the worst of Sam's life. One of the excellent doctors at Mount Weather set his broken nose yesterday, but of course it's killing him today. Pain killers would be nice, but Sam won't take them before meeting Maybe Taylor this afternoon. Pain killers could fog his brain, and he'll need his wits if he's going to talk Maybe into flying back east to kill Sherry Cherry.

Sam hadn't considered he might feel severe pressure building up in his nose as the plane begins its initial descent into Las Vegas, but that's exactly what happens. To make matters worse, his swollen nose has blocked his nasal passages and made him congested to the point his ears feel like they're going to explode.

He tries not to cry out in pain, but he's aware his dull moaning noises are annoying the passengers around him. He dabs at his nose with a cocktail napkin. Within seconds, it's soggy with blood.

disgusting

"That's abhorrent!" the lady next to him says. "You need to do something!"

"Sorry," Sam says.

"Are you crying?" she says.

"Probably."

The pain in his face and ears is excruciating, and blood's dripping from his nose faster than his napkin can contain it. Sam looks up to see the fasten seat belt sign lit and knows the flight attendants are buckled in for the landing. He asks the passengers around him if anyone has an extra cocktail napkin he can use, but either they didn't hear him, or pretend not to. The lady next to him says, "That's just great," and fishes two tampons from her purse.

"It's all I've got," she says. "Do not bleed on my outfit."

Sam accepts the tampons gratefully, opens them, and inserts one into each nostril as expertly as if he'd done it a hundred times.

"I hope you get toxic shock syndrome," she says.

Sam packed light, so he doesn't have to wait at baggage claim. He moves his jaw from side to side and pulls on his ears, trying to open them up. He gets one open in time to answer his cell phone.

"Where the hell have you been?" Darwin says.

"I just landed in Vegas. What's wrong?"

"Donovan Creed is ruining your plans."

"What do you mean?"

"He landed in Roanoke two hours ago."

"Why's that a problem?"

"Check your messages. I've left three."

Sam makes his way to a quiet area and leans against the wall. "Since you're already on the phone, can you just explain the problem?"

"Roanoke is near Creed's headquarters, Sensory Resources. The place you met Doc Howard. The place they kept you after your snake bite. Does any of this ring a bell?"

"Of course. So what?"

"Don't you think Creed might be there to check on Sherry Cherry? To see if she's sobered up enough to effect the exchange?"

"Shit!"

"That's the response I'm looking for."

"If he's got her, it's over. I've lost."

"Not necessarily. He still has to make arrangements with the government, and that will take time. Since you're in Vegas, get Maybe Taylor on board. I'll see if I can arrange for Sherry to escape."

"Thanks."

"Don't thank me, just do your part."

Chapter 20

Maybe Taylor.

MAYBE CALLS SAM from the lobby and learns he's on the second floor, room 228.

She's excited to see Sam. Not because she finds him attractive, or even appealing, but because he adores her so. It allows her to dictate the terms of their relationship. She loves having sexual power over a man, especially a bright, older man like Sam. The fact he's married adds to the appeal. She's flattered he prefers her to his wife, and flattered to hear he's willing to get a divorce to prove his love.

"You look like shit," she says, when he opens the door.

"You look wonderful," he says.

She enters, he closes the door, and slides the deadbolt into place.

"I killed Gwen," she says.

"What?"

She laughs. "Just kidding. But I've got a plan, depending on the weapon you've brought. I've invited her to go shopping with me tomorrow, and—"

"There's been a change of plans," Sam says.

"What do you mean?"

"We need to put Gwen on hold."

"No. I've got it all worked out, and you promised me the money."

"I'll still give you the hundred grand. It's just...there's a different target."

"I'm not killing Callie Carpenter," Maybe says.

"Not Callie. A woman from Virginia."

"What woman?"

"Sherry Cherry."

"What? Don't fuck with me, Sam."

"No, seriously, that's her name. Look, it's no big deal. She's like a housewife or something. It'll take you five minutes. Five minutes for a hundred grand."

"Details, please."

Sam hands her a small metal cylinder. It's silver, and has the words "Lens Cleaner" printed in black on one side.

"Don't open it," Sam says. "It contains a mixture of cyanide and DMSO."

"What's that?"

"Dimethyl sulfoxide. You can use this to kill Sherry and Gwen. But you need to do Sherry first."

Maybe scrunches her nose. "Cyanide's a poison. What do you do, spray it in her nose?"

"Nose, mouth, eyes, are the best targets. But anywhere on her face will work, if you pump it several times. But be careful.

Hold your breath while spraying, and move away quickly. If you do it outside, be sure there's no wind to blow it back into your face."

"How long does it take to work?"

"Seconds."

"Bullshit."

"I wouldn't pay you a hundred grand to kill someone, and provide an inferior weapon," Sam says. "But you can use a gun or knife on Sherry if you'd prefer."

"I'll try the spray, but I want a gun with a silencer as a backup," Maybe says.

"I can arrange that."

Maybe frowns. "Here's what I don't understand. You know all about these poisons. You can arrange for me to get weapons with silencers. Why don't you meet Sherry Cherry yourself and give her face a quick spray?"

"That would deny you the opportunity to earn an easy hundred grand."

"You think I like the killing, don't you?"

"I know you do."

"What prevents me from spraying you in your sleep tonight?"

"Nothing. But you don't have to wait for me to fall asleep. You can spray me right now, if it pleases you."

She looks at the spray bottle. "If this really works, I could kill Callie."

"Test it on Sherry for a hundred grand. Use it on Gwen or Callie, either one, and I'll give you another hundred grand."

Maybe drops the cylinder in her handbag. "What happens now?"

"We make love, and I give you the down payment."

"How about you give me the down payment first?"

"As you wish."

He crosses the floor to the closet, opens his carry-on case, removes ten bank envelopes, and hands them to her. She opens them one at a time, noting they're filled with hundred dollar bills.

"Fifty thousand dollars," Sam says.

Maybe smiles. "When do I go?"

"I'd like you to go with me first thing tomorrow morning."

"I can do that."

"What will you tell your father?"

"I don't need to tell him anything. He's in Louisville."

"You're sure about that?"

"No. But that's where he went last night."

"You haven't heard from him today?"

"Nope. He thinks I'm staying with Callie."

"What did you tell her?"

"I said I was going out for the evening and told her not to wait up for me."

"Good."

"So, you're going with me?" she says.

"Yes. I'll be right by your side when Sherry shows up. But we can discuss the plan after."

"After we have sex?"

"Yes."

"What about room service?"

"We can order whatever you want. After sex."

"What if I don't want to have sex with you?"

"It'd break my heart, but I'd accept it."

"I'm glad to hear that, because I don't want to have sex with you."

"Why not?"

"It would disgust me."

"I don't believe you."

She laughs. "It's easy enough to prove!"

"But I came all this way! I flew six hours with a broken nose and bled all over myself! I haven't taken any pain killers all day just so I could enjoy your body! Not to mention I just paid you fifty thousand dollars!"

"You said if I didn't want to have sex with you, you'd accept it."

"Well, I can't."

"Then why'd you say it?"

"I was bluffing. I need you."

"Sex with me is that important to you?"

"Yes, of course!"

"What's it worth, specifically?"

"What do you mean? You want me to pay you for sex?"

"My father pays women for sex."

Sam considers her comment before saying, "I just gave you fifty grand!"

"That's for killing Sherry Cherry. Not buying sex."

"You'd actually charge me?"

"Yes, of course."

"Why?"

"To prove you're not using me."

"But you'd be using me!"

"I'm okay with that."

Sam gives her a sullen look. "If that's the way you feel about it, charge me now."

"No. I have something else in mind."

"What's that?"

"I want to humiliate you."

He looks bewildered. "I'm sitting here in severe pain with a broken nose. I cried in public today in front of a dozen passengers and crew members and stuffed tampons up my nose, just for the chance to be with you. I've pledged my love and received nothing from you in return. You've reduced me to begging for sex, and I have begged you, and even offered to pay you for it."

"Your point?"

"You think I'm not humiliated enough already?"

"Not even close."

Sam sighs. Pretending to be lovesick over a psychotic killer just to punish her father is beginning to test his limits.

"What do I have to do?" he says.

Maybe smiles.

Chapter 21

Donovan Creed.

I'M IN LOU'S office, viewing sensitive information he's uncovered about Darwin's activities. Every file and document in Lou's office is classified, so I had to ask Miranda to wait in the lobby.

Here's the thing about Lou's information: it's convincing.

Here's the problem: it's too convincing.

For twenty years none of us have been able to find a scrap of information about Darwin. Now, suddenly, Lou has uncovered reams of proof that my old friend, Doc Howard, was monitoring my flights, bugging my office, capturing keystrokes on my office computer, and tracking my movements through my cell phone.

You want to hear the most damning evidence? You'll love this. Doc Howard had five tiny lights installed in every room on the main floor and basement of his house. Lou and I have had one phone number for Darwin all these years, but they were different numbers. When Lou calls, his name shows up on Doc Howard's cell phone, and a blue light goes on in Doc Howard's office and home. When I call, a red light flashes. Lou says if I'll go with him to Doc Howard's office and home, he can prove it to me.

I tell him I don't need to see it.

"Why not?"

"Because I trust you, Lou."

"Right."

The real reason is I already knew about Doc Howard's lights. I've been to his house several times. The first time I visited, he showed me how the lights blink when different people call. But they blinked when I called Doc's number, not Darwin's. If Doc's lights are now blinking when I call Darwin, Lou or someone else has had them reprogrammed.

So I don't buy it.

Doc was a crusty curmudgeon who complained about everything in his life. He ran the infirmary and surgical center at Sensory, and was involved in my facial reconstruction. "Under orders from Darwin," as Doc put it, he implanted a chip in my brain while I was in a coma. But years later, Doc tipped me off about the chip and taught me how to disable it. For this information he charged me a hundred million dollars.

 Lou doesn't know it was Doc who told me about the chip. Nor is he aware of the financial arrangement I made last year with Darwin and Sal Bonadello, the two people most likely to kill me.

I secretly pay them for protection.

Every month my Swiss bank transfers a multi-million dollar payment to two numbered accounts. One is owned by Sal Bonadello, the other, Darwin. The amount is equal to the monthly interest on two five hundred million dollar certificates of deposit.

If I die, the payments stop.

If Sal dies his payment stops.

If Darwin dies, his payment stops.

So both men have a vested interest in keeping me alive.

I'll know in a week if the payment to Darwin has been made. If it has, Darwin's alive. Or at least his eyes are alive. You see, he has to log in with a retinal scan to accept the money.

I don't believe Darwin would have told me about the chip for any amount of money, because that was his insurance against me. Darwin ordered the chip placed in my brain so he could press a button from anywhere in the world and kill me if I ever became a problem.

Thanks to Doc Howard's information, I disabled the chip. So I'm having a hard time believing he was Darwin.

Which means Lou killed the wrong man.

"Callie thinks you're Darwin," I say.

Lou does a double take. "That's crazy! Why would she think that?"

"You and Doc are the two people who claimed Darwin was trying to kill me. And you're the one who uncovered the evidence against Doc. And you're the one who killed him."

"It's logical I found the evidence," Lou says. "It's my research team. Plus, I worked right here in the same building with Doc Howard for more than ten years. If I'm wrong, why was Doc Howard tracking your movements and monitoring your flights? Why would a government surgeon do that?"

"The obvious answer is he wouldn't. But Callie might remind me that you're a computer genius. You gave us fake ID's and wiped our paper trails clean. You've doctored our birth certificates and created diplomas and certifications that prove we're lawyers, doctors, nuclear inspectors, and anything else we need to prove out in the field. For a guy like you, framing Doc Howard would be child's play."

"You know damn good and well I'm not Darwin!" he says.

"You're right."

Lou looks relieved. "You do know?"

"Yes."

"For certain?"

"Of course."

"Then please tell me why. I haven't slept for days, worrying you might come after me."

"Remember when we did the sting together and stole all that money from Sam Case's clients?"

He nods.

"You tried to kill me."

He hangs his head. Then looks up and says, "I don't understand."

"You tried to kill me by pumping the air out of the Lucite container."

"So?"

"I didn't know it at the time, but Darwin ordered a chip planted in my brain years earlier."

"When you were in a coma," Lou says.

"That's right. If you were Darwin, you would've known about the chip. You could've killed me instantly by simply pressing a button."

"Thank God I tried to kill you!" he says.

We look at each other and laugh.

He adds, "Well, you know what I mean!"

I do know. But while I know Lou isn't Darwin, I also know he can't be trusted. He may or may not believe Doc was Darwin. He may or may not be helping the real Darwin frame Doc.

Lou says, "You're having a hard time accepting Doc Howard as Darwin."

"I'm keeping an open mind."

"Want to see his death?"

"You have photos?"

"Video."

As he punches some numbers into his computer I ask, "What, no popcorn?"

"It's a short clip."

He's right. The Doc Howard death video shows Lou killed Doc the old fashioned way. Grabbed him from behind, stuck a syringe in his neck, pushed the plunger.

"Doc and I were very close," Lou says. "I made sure he didn't suffer."

"Why hasn't his death been announced?"

"I'm rewriting his life."

"Not just erasing it?"

"No. I want Doc to have the legacy he deserves. It's easy for us to erase a person's history. But it takes time to create the proper references, letters, public appearances, contributions, and accomplishments a distinguished man like Doc Howard would have made to the world."

"Isn't Ethel asking about her husband's whereabouts?"

"No."

"Because?"

"I'm afraid Ethel suffered an overdose."

I frown. "You couldn't find it in your heart to spare her?"

"Doc was a good husband. Almost never worked late. We're still days away from fixing his background. She would've raised a stink."

"What about Homeland?"

"I informed them of his heart attack this morning. They agree I should keep him on ice till we've cleaned his history."

"Do they know about Ethel?"

"They think she's here at Sensory, under a doctor's care."

"You're holding both bodies?"

"I am."

"Show me."

Lou takes me to the cooler and shows me the bodies. I don't know Ethel well enough to positively identify her, but this other one is definitely Doc Howard. We use a lot of body doubles in our business, but this is my old friend. I'd stake my life on it.

The question remains. Was he Darwin?

"Someone at Homeland knows Darwin's identity," I say.

"You'd think so."

"If they think Doc was Darwin, they'll want to replace him."

"That's my hope."

It dawns on me Lou wants the job. If he's framing Doc Howard, here's another motive.

Lou says, "Don't look so surprised. Stranger things have happened."

"You're a computer expert and researcher."

"So?"

"I doubt they'll offer you the job."

"Maybe they'll offer it to you," he says.

I think about that as I head to the lobby to fetch Miranda.

Chapter 22

Miles Gundy.

WHAT DO LITTLE girls and moms like to do?

Little girls take ballet. Moms take barre classes set to music. What do they have in common? Both use ballet barres, the long banister-type railing dancers use for stretching.

Miles pulls into a parking space that offers an unobstructed view of the entrance to Dancing Barre in Memphis. He tunes his radio to the local sixties station, cranks it up, and sits tight for twenty minutes waiting for the instructor to show up for the three-fifteen class. She's early, of course, but not that early. Miles jumps out of his car, grabs the large canvass bag from the back seat, and enters the studio.

The instructor says, "May I help you?"

"I'm from corporate," Miles says. "And you are?"

"Missy Tadasana."

"I know you've got a class at three-fifteen," he says. "If nothing's out of order, I can be out of here in two minutes."

"I don't understand. Who are you, again?"

"Dancing Barre is a franchise," Miles says. "Twice a year we test the facility for cleanliness."

"Ms. Pranayama didn't say anything about this," Missy says.

"We don't schedule our visits, Missy. That would defeat the purpose."

"Well, this studio is spotless. You can tell by looking."

"I'm sure you're right. But I need to run a special cloth over the ballet barre and the floor to check for microbes. You'll want to watch."

"Why?"

"If the cloth turns blue, we've got a problem."

"I should probably call Ms. Pranayama."

"If the cloth turns blue I'll call her myself. Otherwise, I'll be out of here before you get her on the phone. You want to see how it's done?"

"I guess."

She follows him into the room. He places the bag on the hardwood floor, slides the zipper open, and removes two pairs of latex gloves, a spray bottle, and a thick cloth. After donning the gloves, he sprays the cloth with a chemical until it's wet. Then he wipes the entire length of the ballet barre from right to left, sprays the cloth again, and wipes the barre from left to right.

He holds the cloth up for Missy to see.

"No blue," she says, proudly.

He smiles. "This might be the cleanest facility I've ever tested," Miles says.

"Seriously? Wow! Ms. Pranayama will be so happy to hear that. Do we get a certificate or something?"

"I don't think so. But they'll definitely want to mention it in next month's corporate newsletter."

She smiles. "We can post it on the bulletin board."

"That's a great idea!" he says, as he packs his gear.

"Wait. Aren't you supposed to test the floor?" she says.

"If the barre's this clean, the floor will be too." He winks. "I'm scoring you an A-plus."

"That's rare?"

"Extremely. You should be very proud. Be sure to tell your clients."

She says, "Wait. The barre's still wet. Do we need to wait for it to dry?"

"No. I wore the gloves because my hands are sensitive to the fibers in the cloth."

"In case someone asks, how long before the barre dries?"

"Five to ten minutes."

She looks at the clock above the front desk.

"That'll work," she says.

"Nice to meet you, Missy."

"You too."

Miles leaves, thinking, She never even asked my name!

Chapter 23

Donovan Creed.

MIRANDA AND I are ten miles from Roanoke when my phone vibrates.

"Hi Lou."

"Am I on speaker?"

"You are."

He says, "In that case, Miranda can guess, also."

"Guess what?" she asks.

"How many unemployed chemists are recently divorced and have kids?"

"You already know?" Miranda says.

"What can I tell you?" he brags. "My guys are the best."

I say, "In the United States? In this economy? I'd say twelve."

"How about you, Miranda?" Lou says.

"Six."

"You win. Sorry Donovan."

Miranda smiles.

"She's a natural," I say. Then ask, "So you're saying there are exactly six?"

"No. I'm saying she's closer to the actual number than you."

"So how many, altogether?" Miranda asks.

"One. Miles Gundy. And he lost his custody battle last week."

I take Miranda's hand in mine and bring it to my lips.

"Come work for me!" I whisper.

"No!" she whispers.

To Lou I say, "Miles Gundy?"

"That's right. And you're going to love where he lives."

"Tell me."

"Highland, Illinois."

"Why's that a big deal?"

"It's only a four hour drive from Louisville."

"So are a lot of places," I say. "Give me the address."

"Four-Sixteen Atlantic Avenue."

Miranda writes it down.

I ask, "Is this where he lives? Or his wife?"

"Eloise let him keep the house. She and the kids are staying with her sister."

"You have that address?"

"Twelve-forty-two Vincent. Same town."

"Car?"

"Two-year-old Honda Accord. White. License plate 4XT167C.

"And he worked where?"

"Esson Pharmaceuticals, St. Louis."

"What else do you have?"

Lou gives us the other details he's uncovered, Miranda writes it all down. I tell him to let us know the minute he hears anything that could be related to a mass attack on women or children.

"Of course," Lou says. Then asks, "Shall I call Sherm Phillips? Tell him we think Gundy's our urban terrorist?"

I look at Miranda. She shakes her head no.

I ask, "Has the government sounded an alert about the plastic dispensers?"

"Not that I've heard."

"And you'd know, right?"

"I would."

"Then let's don't call Sherm."

He pauses. "You're sure about this?"

"Yes. I personally warned the President. You heard me."

"But still..."

"They'll send a hundred people to his house. You know they'll fuck it up."

"Of course they will. But we'll get credit for identifying him."

"You'll get even more credit if I catch him with the evidence."

"True."

Lou goes quiet. I know what he's thinking.

"Lou, I don't want to be the next Darwin. I'll track Gundy down and kill him. Then you can tell Sherm you isolated this guy as a possible, and dispatched me to check his house for evidence. I'll make it look like Gundy tried to shoot me."

"Be careful going to his house. It might be booby trapped."

"Speaking of booby traps," Miranda says, "How's Sherry?"

Lou sighs audibly. Then says, "You guys make a perfect couple."

When we get to our hotel, I give Miranda the room key and watch her walk to the elevator. Before getting on, she spins around and blows me a kiss. I touch my cheek and pretend it knocks me back. Then I walk down the hall to Dr. P.'s room and knock on the door. When he opens it I say, "Hello, Darwin."

Chapter 24

"THE PROBLEM WITH this business," Dr. P. says, "You can't get out."

"Tell me about it," I say.

We've been talking ten minutes, long enough to go through the whole "How did you know?" phase.

I just knew.

Something had been nagging at me the whole trip out here. Dr. P. was visibly nervous about taking a trip with me until I explained why we were going to Louisville. Once there, he was terrific with the hospital personnel and the Derby State Fair patients. But he was even more nervous about coming to Sensory Resources. He even wanted to book a flight back to Vegas.

Dr. P. was on the team that planted the chip. He was a staple at Sensory before I arrived. So why didn't I suspect him before now?

He didn't seem the type.

Which is exactly how he survived all these years, undetected.

First of all, you'd never expect a world-class surgeon to be a cold-blooded killer or head up a team that gathers intelligence, conducts assassinations, cleans crime scenes, harvests body-doubles, and makes shady back room deals with high-ranking government officials.

I mean, who has the time?

And second, if it could possibly be a world-class surgeon, you'd expect it to be Doc Howard, not Doc Petrovsky. Doc Howard was the crusty, take-charge head of Sensory's hospital and surgical center. He ran the place. Dr. P. was his trusted employee. It hit me while viewing Doc Howard's body. The logical successor to Doc Howard was Dr. P.

But Dr. P. didn't want the job. Didn't even want to step foot in the place.

Why?

Because he's Darwin.

And tired of it.

He wants to do what I've thought about doing a hundred times.

Retire.

In his case, to Vegas, where he can end his years working in a private practice he owns. He possibly hopes to meet someone, have a social life.

He's sitting on the side of the bed. I'm in the straight-back chair by the desk. The curtains are closed. I make a note to avoid hitting the hanging lamp when I stand.

To his credit, Dr. P. didn't bother denying his identity.

"What happens now?" he says.

"I've always wondered if retirement was possible."

"It's not. They always find you."

"They haven't found you yet."

"Well..." he turns his wrists, showing me his empty hands. Implying I found him.

"You framed Doc Howard?"

"Yes."

"Does Lou know you're Darwin?"

"No."

"Who does?"

"No one."

"That's not possible. Washington knows, yes? And someone at Homeland Security."

"The original people knew. I'm speaking of Watkins and Lorber, but they've been dead for years. Sherm Phillips and the others have been on board since 9/11, and they were told from the start that Doc Howard was Darwin."

"Why?"

"Bill Lorber set it up that way to protect the program. He and I felt Doc was expendable. If we screwed up, killed the wrong people, or leaked the wrong information, Doc would take the fall, and we could continue our work."

"Doc was on board with that?"

"Yes, because there was extra money for that contingency. A slush fund was set up in his name, one he could access on the date of his termination."

"To help cope with the possible public disgrace?" I say.

"Something like that."

I smile. Doc was the most money-hungry man I ever met.

"Must've been a hell of a slush fund."

"It was, and still is."

I say, "So the head of Homeland told Sherm Phillips and the others that Doc was to be known only as Darwin?"

"That's right. We set it up that way because Sensory Resources is too valuable to be a political pawn of whichever party controls Congress at any given moment."

"The show must go on," I say.

"Exactly. But when you bought the spa and plastic surgery center and offered me a job, I saw it as a way to put this life behind me."

"You seriously want to run a private surgical center?"

"Very much so."

"You don't need the money."

He smiles. "You've been quite generous."

"I'm sure you were wealthy long before I started paying you."

"I was indeed. But every little bit helps."

"What about my daughter?"

"Kimberly? What about her?"

I watch him carefully while saying, "She's got a benefactor."

"A benefactor," he says.

"That's right. Someone taught her how to kill people, then paid her to kill them. You know anything about that?"

"Yes."

"Was it you?"

"No."

We look at each other a moment, then he says, "You're referring to Sam Case."

"Excuse me?"

"I only learned this very recently," he says.

"What does Sam know about killing?"

"Believe it or not, he's been running a team of assassins for a year."

"Kimberly being one of them."

"Yes."

"Kimberly told me the man who hired her uses a voice-altering device."

"Yes."

"You've used such a device for the past twenty years."

"That's correct."

"Does Kimberly know the voice belongs to Sam Case?"

"Yes."

"Is he posing as a pre-Rapture pet salesman?"

"I don't even know what that means."

"Is Kimberly...dating...Sam Case?"

Without taking his eyes off mine he says, "No. Sam is in Area B at Mount Weather, and hasn't left the facility since day one. I've been monitoring his activities from the moment I learned he hired Kimberly to kill Jonah Toth. You'll remember Toth used to guard Kimberly. When you discharged him from that duty, I put him back on the payroll, posing as a college professor. And before you ask, I don't know how or why Sam selected Toth or any of the other victims."

He lets that sentence hang in the air a minute, but I can tell he knows more than he's saying. He's hesitating because he's concerned how it's going to come across.

I say, "This is a good time to come clean about everything you know, because I'll eventually find the truth. And when I do, I'll hold you accountable for what you've left out."

"I know something about Kimberly, but it's highly sensitive."

"I'll keep that in mind as you tell me."

He takes a deep breath and lets it out slowly. Then says, "I know you're concerned Kimberly might be having sex with Sam. I can tell you emphatically she's not. I know for a fact she's not having sex with anyone."

"Why's that?"

"She has serious issues regarding sex."

I frown. "How serious?"

"She met with a psychiatrist regularly for months, until he was murdered in his office. Are you aware of her condition?"

"No. And I don't want to hear about it from you."

"Fair enough."

"Do you know who she's dating?"

"I think she's making it up about dating a young man."

"That's her cover story for doing hits for Sam Case?"

"I can't say. But if she's dating at all, it's quite recent. And I know nothing about it."

"Rachel heard I slept with a young woman in Vegas."

"Gwen Peters."

"Is there anything about my life you don't know?"

"I don't know if you're going to kill me today."

I allow that comment to hang in the air a long time before saying, "I assume Gwen told Kimberly we had sex, then Kimberly told Sam, and Sam told Rachel."

"That's probably accurate."

"And you believe Sam paid Kimberly to kill people? Without ever meeting her in person?"

"From what I gather, everything took place by phone."

"That's hard to believe."

"Is it? You've worked for me that way for twenty years."

"True. But I was an assassin before you took over Sensory. Kimberly allowed Sam to manipulate her into becoming a killer. How's that possible?"

"Think about it."

I screw up my face and give him my best Curly impression from the Three Stooges: "I'm tryin' to think, but nothin' happens!"

He gives me an odd look. Then says, "Kimberly craves your love and acceptance."

"You're saying she killed people to gain my approval?"

"Of course."

"And somehow Sam knew she would?"

"That's right."

"Does Kimberly know Sam and I have a history?"

"No."

"Sam's turned Kimberly into a killer to punish me?"

"Yes."

"And you know all these things because?"

"I tapped their phones."

"Kimberly and Sam's?"

"Yes."

"And mine?"

"Yes."

"What about Callie's?"

"No one can tap Callie's phone."

"Why?"

"I don't know. If I knew, I'd love to listen in. Wouldn't you?"

"Hell yes."

We're quiet a minute. Eventually he says, "So, are you going to let me live?"

"I could ask you the same question."

He nods slowly. Then says, "You're familiar with the saying Live and let live?"

I'm not happy about the phone tapping. I also don't like the fact he knew about Kimberly and Sam and didn't tell me. Of course, telling me would expose him as Darwin, so I understand it. I also don't like Doc and Ethel Howard being killed just so Dr. P. can retire peacefully. On the other hand, killing Dr. P. won't bring them back.

"Are you out of the phone tapping business?" I say.

"Yes, effective immediately. I'm sick of all the subterfuge. The killing. If you allow the world to believe Doc Howard was Darwin, I can make a clean break. I want nothing more than to run your plastic surgery center. I want to help people."

He looks at me. "I know you understand this, Donovan. I can tell you're getting close to retiring. I only hope you do it before you get to be my age."

"I'd have more money available for my retirement if I don't have to pay your protection fee," I say.

"Yes, of course. If you allow me to live, I would expect the monthly payments to stop."

I think about the women and children at Jeff Memorial in Louisville, whose faces and hands we promised to restore. Dr. P.'s the only surgeon in the world I'd trust to fulfill that promise. Not only that, but running a plastic surgery center in Las Vegas? The breast implant capital of the world? I can't imagine a better way to meet young, beautiful women.

"I'm okay with Live and let live," I say.

He smiles. "Excellent."

"But that doesn't apply to Sam Case."

"I would think not," Dr. P. says.

"I want you to keep monitoring his activities, and report them to me."

"Even the calls between Sam and Kimberly?"

I think about that a minute, and decide Kimberly's entitled to her privacy. I hope to hell she's not sleeping with Sam Case, because if she is, it's a pure manipulation play to punish me. And if she somehow cares for him, it'll be that much harder on her when she learns the truth. I want to know what Sam's up to, but I don't want to intrude on my daughter's private conversations.

Dr. P.'s waiting for my answer. I give it to him.

"Forget about Sam and his activities. I'll deal with him in my own way. You want to make a clean break? Make it. No more wiretaps, listening devices or monitoring of any kind. No more clandestine activities. I'll let you retire in peace. You'll run the surgical center. We'll help those moms and kids from the Derby City Fair attack, and anyone else who comes to us in need."

"Including Las Vegas showgirls?" he says, with a wink.

"Especially them."

Chapter 25

39008 00118309z

I LEAVE DR. P.—slash—Darwin with his thoughts and take the elevator to our room. Miranda lets me in and I dig through my duffel until I find a disposable cell phone. After putting it in my pocket, I get some hotel stationery and a pen from the desk drawer.

I put my finger to my lips and write, I need a favor. Then hand Miranda the pen.

She writes, Name it.

Use my phone to call your mother. Chat till I come back.

She frowns. How long will you be? You know my mom makes me crazy.

Ten minues.

Okay.

You're probably thinking this business with the phone suggests I don't trust Darwin. In general, I do trust him. Not only that, I'm pulling for him to make it. I mean, how wonderful would it be if Darwin becomes the test case, proving it's possible to eventually retire from this business and live a normal life? On the other hand, he's been keeping tabs on a lot of people for a lot of years, and old habits are hard to break. I have a sensitive call to make, and don't want to take a chance Darwin might monitor it.

I wait till Miranda has her mom on the line, and smile at what she's written on the stationery.

You owe me!

I blow her a kiss and head out the door, down the elevator, and find a quiet spot near an outdoor fountain.

Then I call Callie and ask, "Is Maybe with you?"

"Nope. You called it. She bolted."

"Were you able to follow her?"

Callie laughs. "You really need to teach her the basics. She asked to borrow my Jag."

"And didn't stop to consider it might be rigged?"

"Nope. GPS intact, all cameras functional."

I shake my head. "Where is she now?"

"Room 228, second floor, Vega Rouge Hotel."

"Who's she with?"

"I don't know."

"You're sure about the room number?"

"I watched her elevator go to the second floor and stop. Then I had to run the length of the hall to get to the stairs. I made it to the second floor landing and peeked around the corner just in time to see her enter room 228. From that angle I couldn't see who let her in."

"Good job."

"More lucky than good. If she'd gone to the third floor, I might've missed her."

"Put me on hold and call the front desk. Ask them to connect you to Sam Case."

"You're shitting me!"

"I wish."

"How would he—oh, God, Donovan. You should've let me kill him when I had the chance."

"Tell me about it."

Callie sighs. "I'll call. Hold on."

A minute later she says, "There's no record of Sam Case at the Vega Rouge."

"I didn't expect him to use his real name," I say, "but we had to try."

"I thought he was in the bunker at Mount Weather."

"I thought so too."

"Working on a synthetic cure for the Spanish Flu," she adds.

"He might be there. But as it turns out, he's Maybe's employer."

"Sam Case? He's a computer nerd!"

"A computer nerd who's goal in life is to pay me back for destroying his marriage and business."

"So you think they're meeting about a hit?"

"I'd like to think so, compared to what else I'm thinking. But according to Darwin, all the contracts for murder were arranged by phone."

"Did you say Darwin?"

"Yeah. Darwin's alive and well."

"So I was right? Lou Kelly is Darwin?"

"Try Dr. Petrovsky."

"Bullshit!"

"I'm serious."

"Dr. P.? But how did you—"

"I'll tell you later. Let's try another name Sam might be using."

"Go ahead."

"Donovan Creed."

"What? Why would he use your name?"

"Just give it a try. See if I'm registered."

"You want me to talk to him?"

"No. Just see if he used my name. It would be just like him."

"Okay."

She puts me on hold again. Moments later she says, "Bingo."

Callie says, "I can kill him now, once and for all."

I don't respond.

She says, "Donovan?"

"Sorry. I'm still pondering the idea Sam has stolen my identity."

"Your identity?"

"In order to check in, he'd need a credit card with my name on it."

"Wow!"

"Wow, indeed."

Darwin told me Sam hasn't left the bunker. Doesn't mean he's lying. Sam's a genius. He could probably find a way to confuse Darwin for a few minutes when he needs to come and go. It would have been especially easy during the past thirty hours, since Darwin's with me in Virginia, away from all his equipment.

Darwin also said he's positive Kimberly isn't having sex with Sam. He said she's got some sort of sexual issue she's been discussing with a psychiatrist.

My gut tells me Sam's in a hotel room with my daughter, and sexual issues or not, I expect he's found a way to manipulate her into a physical relationship.

The burning question is do I let Callie kill him?

That's the smart play, and she'd love to do it. But there are two problems with that scenario. First, I'd be denying myself the opportunity to torture Sam to death. And second, my daughter's in the room. Kimberly's not in Callie's league, but she's had some training. If she puts up a fight, Callie will have to hurt her. If she pulls a gun or knife, Callie will have to kill her.

"What do you want me to do?" Callie says.

"Are you available to stay there until Kimberly leaves?"

"Yes."

"Okay. When she leaves, subdue him and keep him there."

"You're on your way?"

"I'm on my way."

Chapter 26

Maybe Taylor.

SAM'S PHONE IS buzzing.

"I need to get that," he says.

"Tough shit."

"Maybe, seriously. I need to answer my phone. You've had your fun. Now untie me."

It has been fun, but there's more fun to be had. She looks at the man who's been such a powerful influence on her life the past twelve months. He's on the floor on his side, naked, curled in a fetal position, arms tied behind his back, wrists cuffed. Knees tied, ankles cuffed. A twelve-inch tail of red tubing protrudes from his backside, courtesy of the butt plug she's placed in his rectum. She was in the process of forcing a red plastic ball in Sam's mouth when his cell phone started buzzing.

She opens it, puts it to his ear.

Sam says, "Hello?"

She hears an altered voice coming through the ear piece. With his ear blocking most of the sound, the words aren't clear to her.

But Sam seems alarmed.

He says things like, "No!" and "You're kidding!" and "What're you talking about?" and "You can't quit!" and "What's going to happen to me?"

Maybe's heard enough. While she enjoys humiliating her boyfriend, no one else is going to upset him on her watch. She pulls the phone from Sam's ear and says, "Who is this?"

Sam screams, "No!"

The person on the other end immediately stops talking, but it's too late. She heard the last few words, and recognized him.

"It's you!" she says.

The voice says, "I don't know what you're talking about."

Maybe says, "I'd know your voice anywhere. Just because it's altered doesn't mean it's different. You called me every day for the past year. Every day until..."

She looks at Sam, sees fear in his eyes. He struggles to break free from the cuffs.

But the cuffs are real.

From some dark place in the pit of Maybe's stomach the anger starts like a smoldering chunk of coal. Within seconds it flares up as if coaxed by a bellows. The flame rises through her body, flushing her neck, ears, and face. Her eyes narrow.

Sam stops trying to break free long enough to say, "Please!"

But the word didn't come from a man's voice. It was more like the sound a whimpering, sniveling little boy might make.

When Maybe speaks into the phone her words are measured, but firm.

She says, "What's going on here?"

The voice on the other end pauses, then says, "I knew nothing about this business with Sam until I heard the tape."

"What tape?"

"Sam had a friend, Doc Howard, who recently passed away. I was going through Doc's things today and came across a tape of a phone conversation he had with Sam a few days ago. I'm going to play you the tape."

And he does.

She stares straight ahead. Blinks twice. Then presses the record button on Sam's phone and says, "Please. Play it once more."

He does.

Then he hangs up.

Then Maybe hangs up.

She looks at Sam, trussed like a turkey.

He whimpers, "I love you!"

She shakes her head, hoping to force her brain to comprehend what she just heard.

"Kimberly!" he says. "What's wrong?"

"You love me, don't you Sam?"

He strains to break the handcuffs on his wrists and ankles, but again, these aren't lovers' toys, they're regulation handcuffs. Sam flops around the floor like the fish she caught many years ago when she was a kid. The fish flipped and flapped and kept trying to hurl itself back into the lake. Eventually the fish gave up and accepted its fate.

Only then did Maybe kick it back into the water.

Sam looks like a trussed turkey when he's not flopping around like a fish out of water. A trussed turkey with a heavily-bandaged beak.

"You love me, Sam?"

"I do! I swear to God!"

"Don't do that."

"What?"

She presses the rewind button and says, "Don't lie to God."

"I wasn't! I was just—"

She presses the speaker button, so he can hear the tape. Without question, it's Sam's voice. And what he's saying is, "Kimberly Creed is inferior to me in every possible way. And now I've made her my fuck pony."

She presses the stop button to observe the effect these words have on her boyfriend.

As she expected, Sam doesn't look so good. His face has turned pale. His lips are trembling.

She presses the play button so Sam can hear his voice say, "Fucking her was child's play! And I'll continue to fuck her as long as it suits me, though she's not much of a lay. If not for the connection to Creed, I wouldn't travel across town to do her."

She's so hurt, so dejected, all she can manage to say is, "Sam."

He says, "I can explain."

But he can't. She sees his mind racing to come up with something plausible to say, but the tape blindsided him so completely he's got...nothing.

She closes Sam's cell phone, tosses it on the bed. Then she walks across the room to retrieve something from her handbag.

He sees it and says, "Don't do this!"

She moves toward him.

Chapter 27

PRISON LIBRARY

Darwin.

DARWIN CAN'T BELIEVE it. Things had been going so well. He called Sam, told him to forget the hit on Sherry Cherry, told him it was too late. Told him, "I'm quitting. I'm out of it."

Then Sam said, "You can't quit!" and Darwin said,  "Creed knows everything. You're on your own!"

Then Darwin said, "If you're smart, you'll take your life before Creed hunts you down."

Except that last part was heard by Kimberly.

Creed's daughter.

The one who thought she'd been talking to Sam for the past year.

Darwin didn't get to age sixty in the assassination business without being quick-witted. He had one ace in the hole.

The tape.

...And figured this was as good a time as any to play it.

127

Perhaps the tape would infuriate her enough to kill Sam. That would be the ideal situation. Because if Sam's alive when Creed shows up, he'll spill his guts and Creed will learn it was Darwin who manipulated Kimberly to become a killer.

Darwin, not Sam.

So he played the tape. She asked him to play it again, and Darwin obliged. Then he hung up and started to make one last call. But before he could press the button on his speed dial, his phone rang.

Creed.

He answers, and Creed says, "Get your things and meet us in the lobby in two minutes. We're out of here!"

Darwin's bags are already packed, which gives him sixty seconds to make one last phone call before his official retirement. The call he's contemplating will impact Rachel Case's future. In Darwin's opinion, Rachel is certifiably insane, and she's Creed's only weakness. He thinks a moment, trying to decide if the call is necessary. For the sake of his partnership with Creed, he decides it is.

When he presses the button, Lou answers.

"This is Lou Kelly. Who's calling?"

Darwin turns on the voice-altering equipment and says, "Lou, this is Holden Prescott.

Lou knows Holden is the chairman of Homeland Security.

Darwin continues, "The committee has reviewed your credentials and are preparing to render a decision regarding your request to replace Darwin. In fairness, I need to point out the committee is divided. Several members feel Donovan

Creed is the best candidate for the job. I happen to disagree. In my opinion, Creed's unstable."

"What can I do to help sway the vote?" Lou says.

"Those who support Creed think you're too soft."

"What? Creed and I worked overseas for years with the CIA. If you check the record you'll see I matched him kill for kill."

"That was a long time ago, Mr. Kelly."

"I'm up for any action that protects my country," Lou says. "Name it."

"There's one thing I know that would sway the committee."

"Tell me. I'll do whatever it takes."

"It has recently come to our attention there's a patient locked away in your facility, in an interior padded cell. She's been receiving drug rehabilitation treatments."

"I'm aware of the patient and the significance of keeping her safe."

"Her safety is no longer an issue."

"I don't understand."

"The Center for Disease Control has gotten to the President. He's nixed the exchange. The scientists at Mount Weather are refusing to give up Rachel Case for Sherry Birdsong."

"Actually, that's good news for me."

"Why's that?"

"As a matter of full disclosure, Ms. Birdsong—who goes by her maiden name, Cherry—has expressed an interest in dating me."

"I'm sorry to hear that, Mr. Kelly, because the government can't afford to let Sherry live. If she's captured by one of our enemies, they could possibly use her genetic code to create the Spanish Flu virus. You want to be head of Sensory Resources? I believe the job is yours, provided you can assume credit for terminating Ms. Birdsong."

"Surely there must be a better way! Have you considered placing her in the bunker at Mount Weather? She's the perfect backup in case something happens to Rachel. You could protect her there, and harvest her genetic code along with Rachel's."

Darwin pauses, then says, "Perhaps the committee is right."

"Sir?"

"Perhaps you aren't emotionally equipped to handle the requirements of the job."

"Wait!" Lou says. "I'll do whatever it takes. Just to be clear, you're saying if I terminate Sherry Cherry, I get Darwin's old job?"

"I can't speak for the rest of the committee, but you'll certainly get my vote."

"What sort of proof will you require?"

"Her hands and head."

"Both hands?"

"Yes."

"How long do I have?"

"Minutes, not hours."

"Count on me," he says.

Darwin hangs up, thinking whatever happens, happens.

He tosses the voice-altering device in the trash, grabs his cell phone, suitcase, and doctor's bag, and heads for the lobby.

From this point on, whether he lives or dies, he'll do so as a civilian.

Chapter 28

Lou Kelly.

SHERRY CHERRY WANTS Lou to sneak her out of Sensory Resources. She wants to go to dinner in Roanoke, someplace fancy. Then she'd like to spend the night with Lou in a nice hotel. Lou would like to do those things, too.

But he also wants to be head of Sensory Resources.

As Lou sees it, there are three issues. One, he's fallen for Sherry, and wants her to be a big part of his life. Two, the chairman of Homeland Security has ordered her death. Three, Donovan Creed has ordered him to protect her at all costs.

If he lets Sherry live, he loses the Sensory job, and Creed will eventually bully the committee, the CDC, and the President himself into putting Sherry in the bunker in exchange for her loony tunes daughter, Rachel. If Lou kills Sherry, Creed will probably try to kill him. On the other hand...

Is there another hand?

Yes.

As head of Sensory Resources, Lou can discharge Creed, put a bounty on his head, and double the security around Sensory until Creed is terminated.

It's not a great hand, but it's the one he intends to play. He cringes, thinking about putting a bounty on Creed's head. There are only so many times you can attempt to kill Donovan Creed and expect to live.

Lou's been told by Holden Prescott he has minutes, not hours, to kill Sherry. But if he disconnects his phone, Prescott will assume he's killed her and is busy disposing of her body.

Lou has every intention of being busy with Sherry's body. It's the least he can do. Give Sherry a nice evening and cap it off with one last round of sex before taking her life.

He doesn't look forward to cutting off her head and hands, though.

Chapter 29

Donovan Creed.

I'M ON THE jet with Miranda and Dr. P., heading back to Vegas, where I have every reason to believe my daughter is holed up in a hotel room with Rachel's husband, Sam Case. There's a slight chance she could be in there with some random guy, but I don't believe a random guy would have booked the room in my name.

I'd call Kimberly, but I don't want to take a chance on losing Sam. If she's fallen for him, she might tip him off and help him escape.

The jet we're in has four captain's chairs, two facing forward, two back. There's also a sofa and table just aft of the chairs. Two additional captain's chairs rest against the back wall where the carry-on bags are stored. Behind that is a full-sized bathroom.

I'm riding backwards, in one of the captain's chairs, facing Miranda. Dr. P. is semi-reclining on the sofa, facing me.

He's either napping, or pretending to nap. He told me Sam hasn't left the bunker at Area B. Either that's a lie, or Sam found a way to leave and re-enter Area B undetected.

I don't think Dr. P. is lying about Sam. If he truly wants to retire from the business, why bother lying about Sam?

We're at 40,000 feet now, and there's no way Dr. P. can listen in on my calls while I'm watching him.

I call Callie.

"Hi boss," she says.

"What's up?"

"Same old. Can you talk?"

"Yes."

"She's still in there."

"Have you gotten close enough to listen?"

"No. I don't know how extensive her training has been, but if I'm close enough to hear, I'm close enough to be noticed through the peep hole."

"Where are you?"

Callie laughs. "Down the hall, in the cubby with the ice machine. I'm using my makeup mirror to keep an eye on the room."

"And Gwen?"

Callie sighs. "Gwen's texting me to death. I'm either going to have to get a new girlfriend or get out of the business."

"The pretty ones are always high maintenance," I say, noting the smirk on Miranda's pretty face. She glances behind her to make sure she's not being watched, then lifts her tank top and gives me a double.

I smile, enjoying the view. She allows me five seconds of entertainment before putting the twins back to bed.

134

Callie says, "I can think of a dozen ways to get in their hotel room. And all of them involve eating a sandwich while watching the Dani Ripper thing on TV. After I tie Sam and Maybe to their chairs, of course."

"I'll bring you some fries," I say. "In the meantime, eat ice."

"Forget the fries. You're buying me and Gwen a steak dinner at Switch."

"She'll eat steak?"

"On steak day."

"She has a steak day?"

"Steak day, fruit day, smoothie day, vegetable day, sweet day—how many is that?"

"Who gives a shit?" I say.

"Good point."

She pauses, then says, "Remember the last time we went there?"

"Switch?"

"Yeah."

"I do. A lot's happened since then."

We go quiet while I think about Kathleen and she thinks about Eva.

Finally she says, "I'll let you know if something changes."

"Thanks."

I look at my watch. We're three hours from Vegas.

Miranda says, "Can I buy a few things when we land?"

"I won't have time. But I'll get you a car and driver and give you a credit card."

"Where are we staying?"

"Vega Rouge."

"That's the one with the big mall and cool restaurants?"

"I think so."

"And you're going there straight from the airport?"

"I am."

"Then I'll go with you!" she says. "I can check in for us and shop till you call me."

"Sounds like a plan," I say.

"How many days will we be together?"

"As many as it takes to catch Felix."

"Can you catch him within a week?"

"You've got a whole week?"

Miranda smiles. "For you? Yes."

"In that case, I'll catch him quickly. Then we'll go somewhere fun."

"Where?"

"Let's ask the twins."

She lifts her top again, gives her torso a shake.

I love hanging out with the twins.

Chapter 30

Miles Gundy.

THE HSV-1 VIRUS is one of Miles's favorites. This is the basic cold sore virus most people contract before age six. When the cold sore goes away, the virus remains in the body for life, appearing from time to time for no predictable reason.

There's no permanent cure for HSV-1.

It's contagious, and spreads through direct contact, as Miles learned four months ago when combining it with the highly toxic agent, dimethylmercury. On that occasion he spilled a single drop on his gloved hand. As a result, Miles is dying. The only reason he's still alive? He immediately underwent treatment for mercury poisoning.

Upon contact, Dimethylmercury enters the bloodstream and slowly works its way to the brain. It generally takes four months to notice the first symptoms, but when it comes, it's quick. Your speech slurs, you drop things, you stumble into walls. Three weeks later, you die.

But by combining the poison with the live HSV-1 virus, Miles created a toxic stew that will enter the skin of anyone who touches the barre for the next two hours. Because the Dancing Barre ladies are exercising, it's only a matter of time before they'll wipe the sweat from their eyes, noses, or mouths, at which point Miles's concoction will enter their mucous membranes. The ladies will be symptom-free for ten days, but they'll die four days later.

Two weeks from now, when doctors realize the instructor and every member of the 3:15 p.m. exercise class died on the same day, people all over the country will fear exercise classes.

It would be nice to think his concoction would have far-reaching effects, where one infected person would infect ten, and those ten would infect ten more, but it doesn't work that way. The entire life cycle of the contagion is about four and a half hours, meaning, anyone not infected by 7:30 pm tonight will be safe. What's worse, only about five percent of infected people will prove to be carriers of the disease.

That is not to say Miles hasn't made an impact.

Take Joy Adams, for example. Joy reserved the last spot for the 3:15 p.m. exercise class at Dancing Barre. After class, she'll catch a plane to visit her sister in Roanoke, Virginia. She'll hold her boarding pass in her contaminated hands and pass it to the gate attendant, who'll be dead fourteen days later. On the plane, Joy will touch the arm rests, the tray table, the overhead compartment latch, her water bottle, her drink glass and napkin, the in-flight magazine, and any number of other items. Until about 7:30 p.m. some or all of those items will be infected, and the chances are high at least another dozen people will come into contact with them.

When Joy disembarks her plane, she'll embrace her sister and brother-in-law and their two kids, and their dog. The dog will be fine, but the family won't. That night, they'll take her out to dinner at Chez Villesa, where she'll enter the restroom at 7:23 p.m. After peeing, she'll use the soap dispenser, at which point the virus will have approximately seven minutes to live.

What are the odds the very next woman who touches the soap dispenser will be that one-in-twenty person who can spread the virus during the final seven minutes?

Chapter 31

Donovan Creed.

TWO HOURS OUT of Vegas, my cell phone vibrates.

"What's happened?"

Callie says, "Maybe just left the room."

"Alone?"

"Yes."

"Perfect. How did she look?"

"Cool as a cucumber."

"Good. You want to try to get in?"

"Yes. If I hurry, he'll probably think Maybe left something behind."

"Let me know when you're in."

"Will do."

We hang up. Five minutes later, Callie calls.

"What's up?"

"No answer."

"You knocked loudly?"

"Yes. And called the room. You think she killed him?"

"No."

"Then what?"

"I think he saw you."

"I don't think so," Callie says.

"Perhaps Maybe came back, saw you knocking, and called him."

"I don't think so."

"Keep an eye on the door till I get there. If he starts to come out, run over, push him back inside, and give me a call."

"I could act like I lost my key, get the maintenance guy to let me in."

"I don't like it. Too many problems. The door might be latched. The maintenance guy might see something. Sam might scream for help."

"Fine. I'll sit tight."

"See you soon."

"By soon, you mean, what? Ten minutes?"

"Ninety."

"Shit."

"Maybe he'll come out soon."

"Hard to come out if he's dead," she says.

"He's not dead. Trust me."

"But he will be soon after you arrive?"

"Not too soon."

"Goody," she says.

Chapter 32

Lou Kelly.

LOU AND SHERRY arrive at Chez Villesa, in downtown Roanoke, at 7:20 p.m., and find the restaurant completely packed. More than a dozen couples are waiting for tables. Lou glances at the bar and sees it's even more crowded than the restaurant. He knows the manager, and tries to bribe him, but what can be done when there are no tables at all?

"How long's the wait?" he asks.

"We're running an hour wait right now." He notices the Franklin in Lou's hand and says, "I can maybe find you something in thirty minutes."

Lou turns to Sherry. "You want to wait or try somewhere else?"

She thinks a moment.

"Let's find something quieter, and more romantic."

Lou smiles. "I agree."

They exit the restaurant and start heading to Lou's car.

Suddenly Sherry stops and says, "Maybe I should use the restroom before we go."

"You sure?"

She says, "I can probably hold it a little longer."

Lou shrugs. "Better safe than sorry," he says.

She kisses his cheek, says, "I'll be right back."

As Sherry opens the door to the ladies' room, a young, fit woman walks out. Sherry pees, then pushes the top of the soap dispenser several times and washes her hands. Then she cups her right hand under the faucet, collects some water, puts it in her mouth, and swirls it around, to freshen her breath. Then she spits it into the sink, checks her hair, and exits the restroom.

Chapter 33

DINNER AT ROMANZA was more romantic than Lou and Sherry could have imagined, and the hotel sex that followed rekindled something in Lou that had been dormant for years. After making love for a surprising second time, Sherry gets up and pads to the bathroom.

Lou decides it's now or never.

He rolls to the side of the bed and sits up with his feet touching the floor. He looks at the bathroom door. For years he's wanted the head job at Sensory. It's as if his entire career was a prelude to this crowning achievement.

All he has to do is open the door, come up behind her, and snap her neck.

He hears her running the water, washing her hands. Living alone all these years, Lou never hears anyone running the water in the bathroom of his apartment.

It suddenly dawns on him that everything he wants is behind that door.

Let Creed or someone else run Sensory. Lou's wealthy enough. Maybe he'll retire and settle down with Sherry. Surely Creed will allow it, especially after Lou explains how the President reneged on the deal to exchange her for Rachel.

The bathroom door opens, and Sherry comes out, wearing nothing but a smile.

"You know what I think?" she says.

"Tell me."

"I think I'm falling in love with you!"

Lou beams.

Sherry tumbles into his arms. They fall back onto the bed, where they remain for hours, cuddling, kissing, and pronouncing their love, totally convinced they'll be happy the rest of their lives, completely unaware they'll be dead in two weeks.

Mercury poison's a bitch.

Chapter 34

Donovan Creed.

AFTER WHAT SEEMS like weeks on the jet, we finally land in Vegas. The pilots rush to get our luggage into the waiting limo, and Miranda and I order the driver to take the short route to the Vega Rouge.

As we're waiting in line to check in, Callie's on my cell phone saying, "If Sam's in room 228, he's dead. There's no sound inside, and he hasn't responded to my phone calls or knocking."

"I agree something's up," I say. "But not that. I'll be there in a minute."

"Bring a strip steak."

Moments later, she sees me coming and pops out from her spot in the cubby. Normally I'd head straight for Sam's door, but hotel guests are walking up and down the hall, entering and exiting rooms.

"Has it been this busy all afternoon?"

"Off and on."

"Feast or famine?"

"Don't say feast to a starving woman."

I enter the little cubical where she spent all those hours. It's basically a small room without a door that contains a standard ice machine, and nothing else. The front of the machine has an opening for your ice bucket. You set it there, press the button, ice falls into the bucket. I notice a drain under the opening where the bucket sits.

I carefully inspect the metal below the opening, then sniff the drain, and look at Callie with curiosity.

She gives me a condescending look and shakes her head as if to say she knows exactly what I'm thinking, and can't believe it.

"I've got to know," I say.

"Of course you do."

"Tell me."

"You're not getting off that easy. Ask the complete question out loud, so you can hear how immature you sound to me."

"Fine. How did you pee all this time? You couldn't have come prepared."

"I always come prepared."

"Prove it."

"How?"

"Open your purse."

"Our generation calls this a handbag."

"Whatever."

She opens her handbag. I glance through it and find no cups, mugs, jars or containers of any kind. I do see her gun.

I return the pretty lady's purse before the guy coming toward us with the ice bucket sees me holding it.

He gets his ice, trying desperately not to stare at Callie. I can tell he's curious about the two of us standing by the ice cubby without buckets. This is where I'd normally expect some hero wannabe to ask, "Miss? Is this man bothering you?"

But he doesn't. Just gets his ice and leaves.

"I don't get it," I say, waiting for him to enter his room and close the door.

She says, "You're still dwelling on the pee thing?"

"Of course. How'd you do it?"

"How would you have peed?"

"I'm a guy."

"Exactly. But you still have to say it."

"Why?"

"Because this is your conversation topic, not mine."

I shrug. "I would have whipped it out and peed directly into the drain below the ice dispenser."

"Of course you would."

"So?"

"That's disgusting."

"A drain's a drain."

"Spoken like a guy who probably pees in the shower."

Ignoring her comment, I say, "So how did you manage it?"

She reaches in her purse and removes a tiny little silver... what's that sewing thing called? Oh yeah. A thimble! She holds it up, proudly. I stare in disbelief.

"That's impossible," I say.

"Not impossible at all. I peed in this till it filled up. Then I drank it."

"Bullshit. First of all, you could never direct your stream into that ridiculous thimble. Second, —why are you smiling?"

"How long have you known me, Donovan?"

"Twelve million years."

"That feels about right. Especially today. And you're an expert on sewing now?"

"Of course not. But I know enough about anatomy to emphatically state you didn't pee in that thimble."

"And if I stubbornly persist in saying I did, what does that make me?"

"I don't know. What, a stubborn idiot?"

"And yet, over the last several hours you've told me Sam Case is in that room, and he's alive, despite all the proof I've offered."

"I know he's in that room. And I know he's alive."

"You know what that room is, Donovan?"

"What's that?"

"Your thimble."

I point down the hall. "Room 228 is my thimble."

"That's right. And your reasoning doesn't hold water."

I wonder how she came up with all that based on me sniffing the drain. I hate it when the people who work for me prove, time and again, how much smarter they are than me.

Callie says, "The coast is clear. So, what now? Want me to call the room?"

"Nope."

"Knock on the door?"

"Nope."

"Find the superintendant? I can distract him while you enter."

"Nope."

She frowns. "We can't kick the door down."

"Follow me," I say, and lead her to the room. When we get there, I stand behind the wall left of the door, and motion Callie to hug the wall to the right. The wall wouldn't protect us from assassins, because professional killers would shoot through the walls first. But if Sam or some other civilian inside starts shooting, we'd expect them to shoot through the door.

Civilian shooters are like college quarterbacks at the start of a big game. Their adrenalin kicks in and they always aim high.

Which is why I motion Callie to go low.

She takes a knee, puts her hand in her purse—handbag— and nods, to let me know she's gripping her gun.

I take a key card from my pocket, reach my arm across the door, slide the card through the lock. It clicks open. I turn the handle and push. The door opens maybe an inch. I take a deep breath, glance at Callie to make sure she's ready to storm the room.

She's not.

She's shaking her head, frowning.

"What's wrong?"

"You've got a key?"

"Think about it."

She does.

Then smiles.

"Sam used your name when checking in. You went to the front desk, showed your ID, told them you left your key in the room. They gave you another key."

"Exactly. Now it's your turn."

"For what?"

"How did you manage to pee all this time?"

Callie rolls her eyes. "Let it go."

"I can't."

"Why not?"

"You're wearing pants."

"Our generation calls them jeans."

"You wouldn't have pulled your jeans off in the hallway. And even if you did, you couldn't have hiked your leg up and hit the drain without dribbling down the front of the ice machine."

"Donovan."

"Yeah?"

"Let's see what's inside the room."

"Okay."

Chapter 35

I PUSH THE door open and duck back behind the wall while Callie gets a view of the room. As the door starts to rebound and close I say, "Good to go?"

"Yes! Bathroom's on the right."

"Be careful!"

Before the door swings shut on its own, Callie pushes it again, and hurls herself past the open area that leads to the bathroom. It's a thing of beauty, watching Callie fly through the air, gun in hand, ready to shoot whoever might be lying in wait. It's a fraction of a second in real time, but when you do what we do, as long as we've done it, time stands still, giving a guy like me time to admire the athletic grace of a truly amazing killing machine like Callie Carpenter. It's like watching Michael Jordan in his prime. You know you're seeing something special, a once-in-a-generation talent.

I come in high, just behind her, running directly toward the bathroom, in case someone's trying to draw a bead on Callie.

But no one's there.

"Bedroom's clear," she says.

"Closet's clear," I say.

I wait for her to retrieve her purse from the hallway. She does, and re-enters the room and closes the door. I'm standing in front of the closed bathroom door. A sitting duck if Sam starts shooting.

I motion Callie to stand out of the line of fire.

She does, but says, "He's being awfully quiet for a live guy."

I call out, "Sam?"

"Before you go in," Callie says, "I'd like to put some money on it."

"You're that sure he's dead?"

"Yes."

I think about it. Everything in my experience tells me Sam's in the bathroom, lying in the tub, unconscious. Of course, this would mean he's been unconscious a long, long time.

Highly unlikely.

But Callie said Maybe was cool as a cucumber when she left. Crimes of passion leave you edgy, and haggard. Not to mention if Maybe had blood on her clothing, Callie would've noticed.

"A hundred says Sam's alive," I say.

"A hundred grand?"

"No. A hundred dollars."

"Make it five hundred," she says.

"Fine."

I turn the bathroom door handle, open the door.

Chapter 36

Callie Carpenter.

CALLIE LOVES WORKING with Creed. When the two of them are together, it adds an element of fun to the job. Plus, they're unstoppable. Whether it's something simple, like charging a hotel room, or huge, like attacking an enemy stronghold, they have the perfect chemistry for orchestrating lethal violence.

Callie loves his quirks!

There's no one on earth she adores more than Creed, though she'd never admit it. She's naturally in tune with him and has been, since the day he brought her into the business.

When he's around, there's nothing she'd rather do than tease or torment him.

Take today, for example. She had all afternoon and evening to think about the best way to fuck with his mind. Being Callie, she managed to come up with five great possibilities. But the one she knew would drive him crazy is if he couldn't figure out how she managed to pee.

Why would it cross her mind in the first place?

Those who follow people for a living, or spend hours staking out homes, hotel rooms, or businesses, know there's nothing more important than having a plan for using the bathroom. How many times has a person escaped surveillance at the exact moment the investigator left his post to find a place to pee?

It never fails.

Creed knows this and knows Callie would never take her eyes off the target. Therefore, he'd expect Callie to have something in her handbag. A large to-go coffee cup with a lid, for example.

Which is exactly what Callie used twice while maintaining her surveillance on Sam's hotel room door.

Knowing Creed would arrive soon, Callie climbed on top of the ice machine, lifted a ceiling tile, and hid her pee cup on top of the adjoining tile. Then she put the first one back in place, dusted the top and sides of the ice machine, to remove any ceiling tile particles that might be visible.

Callie smiles, thinking about it.

Most people would say she's crazy to go to so much trouble to make Creed wonder how she managed to pee while watching a hotel room door. But Callie knows it's the little things, the unexpected, unexplained details—that get under the skin of a man like Creed, and hold his interest.

Like the way he thinks she's a lesbian.

Creed is fascinated by the whole girl-on-girl dynamic.

But Callie's little secret? She's just as comfortable being with a man. Would actually prefer a man, if she could find one she could respect. The reason she dates women? They're easier to find, easier to love. While her looks and strong personality are intimidating to men, they're catnip to women. Cool, sexy, fun women are easy to find because they approach her. And Callie can accept them for who they are. They don't have to measure up to some ideal standard.

And they don't keep score. In other words, if Callie beds both John and Jane Doe, only John will run out and tell all his friends about it. Callie likes to keep her personal life private.

As for men, being around Creed has spoiled her. Of course she's met handsome, powerful men in her life. But none measure up to Creed. After hanging around Superman, could Lois Lane ever be happy with Jimmy Olsen or Perry White?

Of course not!

But Lois could find any number of fun women to date, and it would never cross her mind to compare them to Superman.

The million-dollar question is, could Callie ever fall in love with a man like Creed?

Of course.

She already loves him!

Naturally she has no current plans to reveal her feelings. Not until she's convinced he's ready to settle down. Since Creed's still enjoying the company of hookers, he's not even close to being ready.

Callie stormed the room low, while Creed went high. Good as she is, she would've been nervous diving into a hotel room unarmed. Especially facing a rank amateur like Sam Case, who wouldn't be where he should be, or doing what he should do.

Creed took the high position, unarmed.

God, what a thing of beauty he is! Handsome, confident, willing to put himself in the line of fire to protect her. It was a fraction of a second in real time, but when you do what they do, as long as they've done it, time stands still, giving a woman like Callie time to admire the athletic grace of a truly amazing killing machine like Donovan Creed. It's like watching Mikhail Baryshnikov in his prime. You know you're seeing something special, a once-in-a-generation talent.

He took her breath away. As he does whenever they're together.

But he's wrong about Sam.

Creed says he's alive, Callie says he's dead.

They bet five hundred dollars on the outcome, and now it's time to find out.

Creed turns the bathroom door handle, opens the door, steps inside.

Callie pauses, then cautiously approaches.

Creed's hand becomes visible through the door opening.

He's holding five hundred dollars.

Which means Callie wins the bet.

She plucks the cash from his fingers, stuffs it in the pocket of her jeans, and enters the bathroom.

Chapter 37

Donovan Creed.

SAM'S DEAD.

Callie accepts my money with not a hint of joy or satisfaction. One thing about Callie, there will be no "I told you so's."

She understands my disappointment.

I look at what's become of Sam Case and know I started this.

I stole Sam's wife and ruined his business.

In order to exact revenge, he befriended my daughter, turned her into a killer, and manipulated her into a sexual relationship. I have no idea what occurred between them that would have led her to do this. It would've been fitting and so much more satisfying for Sam and me to end our bitter rivalry in a more personal manner.

Seeing Sam like this, it's hard to picture him as the somber genius and worthy adversary I've learned to grudgingly respect.

He's in the bathtub, naked, tied into a fetal position, looking like some sort of freak show. His arms are tied behind his back, and his wrists and ankles are handcuffed. The scratches on his knees indicate they'd been tied together at some point. She's put eyeliner and eye shadow on his eyes and lipstick on his lips. A red ball has been stuffed in his mouth, held in place with two elastic straps that encircle his head. A red, rubber tube is hanging out of his ass.

"The tail's a nice touch," Callie says, "but she made a mess of his throat. What's that about?"

"She cut his vocal chords so his screams wouldn't be heard."

"She must have knocked him unconscious first, or I would have heard him scream when she started cutting his neck."

"That sounds right," I say. "She probably intended to torture him, but didn't realize he'd choke to death from the blood."

Callie says, "No offense, but she needs more training."

I look at her and say, "No one better for that job than you."

She starts to respond, then changes her mind.

I say, "You've got to admire the fact she did all this and walked out the door calmly."

"No blood on her clothes means she thought ahead," Callie says. "She must have untied his knees, made him hop to the bathtub, then hit him over the head to make him fall in. Then she removed her clothes, cut his neck, and took a shower to scrub his blood off her body."

"I agree. But now we've got a problem."

"How to dispose of his body?"

"That, and the fact this room is in my name."

"Shit, you're right."

"Any ideas?" I say.

"We could call Joe Penny and have him bring us a bomb."

"A bomb."

"That's right. Nothing destroys a crime scene better than a bomb!"

"You'd kill all the innocent people in the rooms around us?"

"Of course not, though I doubt they're all innocent. Joe sets the bomb, and we set off the fire alarm. When the building's completely empty, Joe blows the room to hell, and no one's the wiser about Sam."

"Or we could just remove his body and clean up the blood."

"But the room's in your name," Callie says.

"Right, and I checked into a second room a few minutes ago. Miranda can stay in that one tonight, I'll stay here, clean this one, and keep the housekeepers out.

"But the actual body?"

"Darwin's retired, but he still has a contact list."

"You're a hundred percent positive Dr. P. is Darwin?"

"I am. Believe it."

She chuckles.

"What?"

"Yesterday you were going to kill him. Now you're going into business with him?"

"I know. Funny, right?"

"You're keeping him alive for the boob jobs."

"What?"

"You hope to meet show girls."

"Are you serious?"

"Don't protest too loudly. You'll just embarrass yourself."

"Okay."

We stand there a while, looking at what's become of Sam Case.

"He was the most brilliant man I ever met," I say.

Callie says, "Can I order room service now?"

Chapter 38

CALLIE ORDERS ROOM service, and I call Dr. P.

"See what I mean?" he says. "You can never get out of this business."

"It's just one last body," I say.

"Someone you know?"

"Sam Case."

He pauses. Then says, "You're certain?"

"Quite. No one shits rubber tubing like Sam."

"I have no idea what that means," Dr. P. says, "but if he found a way out of Area B without me knowing it, he's managed to defeat my surveillance."

"Don't beat yourself up about it," I say. "He's dead and you're out of the business."

"Which is why I can't personally call the cleaner."

"Good point. Give me the contact info, and I'll deal with him personally."

"Her."

"What?"

"My Las Vegas cleaner's a woman."

"You're kidding!"

"She's a former crime scene investigator, fallen on hard times."

"But trustworthy?"

"Completely."

He gives me her name and number.

Nelia Mitchell thanks me profusely for calling.

"When I heard Darwin passed, I thought I'd never work again!" she says. "Thank God you got my number! You think you can keep me busy for the next few years?"

I like her attitude.

"I'll do my best," I say.

"God bless you, Mr. Creed."

I do meet some strange people in this business.

"I'll need specifics," she says.

"Like what?"

She chuckles. "You're new at this, aren't you?"

"The cleaning up part? Yes, ma'am. What do you need?"

"Is the victim a man or woman?"

"Man."

"Height?"

"Six feet, more or less."

"Exact is better."

"Why?"

"We're going to wheel him out of there in a suitcase. Be a shame if his head is sticking out."

"Say six feet, then."

"Weight?"

"One eighty-five."

"How much blood?"

"Confined to the bathroom floor, the tub, and splash tiles. There's probably some on the shower floor and in the drains."

"We'll take care of the drains."

"We?"

"I'm an old lady. I can't do all this by myself."

"Let's be clear. I deal with you, you deal with the crew."

"No one sees you but me," she says.

"When can you be here?"

"Vega Rouge? Give me two hours."

"Thanks, Nelia."

"Don't thank me, pay me."

"How much?"

"For this job? Eight grand."

"That sounds high."

"How much would you pay a lawyer to keep you out of jail?"

"Good point."

"Cash, honey."

"Yes, of course."

"In advance."

"Yes ma'am."

Chapter 39

MY NEXT CALL is to my daughter, Kimberly.

"Maybe Taylor," she says.

"Are you okay?"

"Of course. Why do you ask?"

"I'm in a hotel room with a dead guy."

"That's got to be more fun than you're making it sound."

I try to keep the smile out of my voice as I ask, "Where are you?"

"Out drinking. But don't worry, I'm not driving. I've got a hotel room upstairs."

"Not the room where I'm standing, I hope."

"Nope. I'm down the street."

"You're drinking you say?"

"Uh huh."

"Got troubles?"

"I broke up with my boyfriend tonight."

"Yeah. That's sort of why I called."

"I know."

"You want some company?"

"Tomorrow? Sure. But not tonight."

"But you'll be okay?"

"I will."

"Because?"

"I've got a great job, working with my dad."

"Your dad sounds very handsome."

She giggles. "He is."

We're quiet a while.

Then I ask, "Anything you want to say to me?"

"Yes."

"Go ahead."

"Don't tell Mom what I did, okay?"

"Okay."

Chapter 40

ME, TALKING TO Callie: "Room service was a great idea."

"I agree," she says, "I'm totally starving."

"You know how I knew that? The four pounds of food you ordered."

She flips me the finger.

Undeterred, I say, "Sam's tucked away in the bathroom."

"So?"

"The room service guy saw us here together, cool, calm, collected. We let him take his time setting the table and so forth."

She cuts into her tenderloin and says, "You mean it establishes we didn't kill a man, hack his vocal chords out of his neck with a pocket knife, or stick a tube up his ass."

"Exactly."

When Callie takes a bite of her steak I'm reminded how much I love watching her eat. She's truly stunning. Crazy

167

as it sounds, the way she moves her mouth when eating is something I'd pay money to see. Of course, I'd pay more to see what's going on under those jeans. My mind suddenly shifts to Callie in the cubby with the ice machine, pulling her pants down enough to pee.

"Will I get to meet Miranda this trip?" she says.

"Excuse me?"

"Miranda. Do you have plans to introduce us?"

"You want me to?"

"Sure."

"Then I will."

I think about it a minute, then say, "What made you ask that?"

"About Miranda? You were staring at me."

"I was?"

"At my lap, if we're being precise."

"You're sure about that?"

"It's a chick thing. We know when you glance, we know when you stare. You weren't glancing."

She takes a bite and adds, "You stared at my face, then my boobs, then my crotch. With extreme lust."

"Extreme?"

"Again, a chick thing. There are degrees of lustful stares. Yours was extreme."

"Can you blame me?"

She swallows her steak, cuts another wedge. "Blame you? Explain."

"Christ, Callie, you're gorgeous. Your body makes me crazy! You're literally the most beautiful woman I've ever seen. And I've told you that a million times."

168

"And I'm always pleased to hear it. But your problem with women?"

"Do tell."

"You're lazy."

"I have no idea what you're talking about."

"Gorgeous women require extra effort. In a choice between a gorgeous woman, and a willing one, you'll settle for willing every time."

"Well hell, what man wouldn't?"

"What man indeed."

I say, "Miranda is not only willing, she's beautiful and brilliant."

"What're you saying? She might be the one?"

"No, of course not. But can I ask you something?"

"Sure."

"Why are you being so catty tonight? I'm far more selective than you're making it sound. Surely you can imagine how hard it is to find women who'll accept my lifestyle."

She pauses, then says, "You're right. I'm sorry. I had no idea Miranda was that important to you."

"Well, she is."

"You really care for this lady?"

"I do. Very much. And thanks for not calling her a hooker."

"You're welcome. But...if she's here, and she's so special to you, why were you staring at me just now?"

"Because you're Callie Carpenter!"

"This is a compliment, yes?"

"Definitely. You're one of a kind. I'd give anything to have you."

"As a man who employs hookers, is this the point where you make me an offer?"

I look at her, looking at me. If there's one woman in the world who could get me to settle down, it's this one. Not only is her beauty unsurpassed, she's everything I seek in a woman. Callie's the total package. She completes me.

In short, we're perfect together.

We work well, enjoy the same things. Like making money, shopping, killing bad guys, watching movies, going to theater, sleeping with beautiful women, and millions of other things, like...

"I look forward to it."

"Excuse me?"

"Meeting Miranda," she says. "I can't wait to meet her."

I frown. "Fine. I'll introduce you now."

"Fine," she says.

I get Miranda on the phone and ask, "Are you up for meeting a friend of mine?"

"Of course. When?"

"Right now. I'm in room 228."

"Give me ten minutes. I'm still in the mall."

"See you then."

I click the phone off.

Callie says, "She's going to be angry."

"Miranda? No way."

I pause a moment, then say, "Why would you think that?"

"You brought her to Vegas to be with you, then sent her to the mall to shop. That's very sexist, making her shop alone."

"Well excuse me, Gloria Steinem, but I've been rather busy just now, discovering and trying to figure out how to dispose of a dead body and clean up a crime scene. I suppose the politically correct thing would be to bring a date to the next killing."

"No need to get defensive."

"How could I not? You just accused me of treating Miranda badly."

"You probably told her you had business to attend to."

"That's right."

"Now she's going to come to the room and see an unmade bed, and the two of us sitting alone in a hotel room, having dinner together."

"It's not like Miranda and I are a couple."

"Are you kidding me?" Callie says.

"About what?"

"She's a woman, Donovan, and...wait. Do I really need to explain this to you?"

"Yes."

Callie puts her fork down, gets to her feet, and sighs. "Look. I don't care what you're paying her. If she's as nice as you say, she's probably got feelings for you. And if so, she's going to feel slighted."

"Slighted?"

"Insulted. Hurt. Abandoned."

Callie knows I have abandonment issues.

"You added that last part for my benefit," I say.

"Everything I said was for your benefit, Donovan."

I think about that a minute. Then say, "Why do you care if I hurt Miranda's feelings?"

She shrugs.

"What's that mean?"

"I'm a woman."

"When one suffers you all do?"

She gives me an odd look, like maybe I said something intelligent by mistake. She shakes it off and says, "I'm your friend, Donovan. I care about you. I want you to be a better man."

We look into each others' eyes. As always when that happens, a surge of warmth floods my body.

Callie says, "Call her back. Tell her to finish shopping. Say you'll meet her in your other room in an hour. By then the cleaner will be here."

"Then what?"

"Wait for her to take a long, hot shower. Let her get all dolled up and have her put on one of her new outfits. When she does, tell her she's so beautiful she takes your breath away."

"Then what?"

"Then drive her to my place to meet me and Gwen. She'll think we're pretty, but she won't feel threatened."

"Why would she feel threatened in the first place? She's a hooker!"

"She's a woman, Donovan, a woman with deep feelings for you. She wouldn't give you this much of her time if you weren't important to her."

"Anything else?"

"While you're at my place don't show Gwen or me the slightest interest. Dote on Miranda the entire time. Brag on her. Be proud of her in front of us. If Gwen happens to make a snotty remark, defend your lady. That'll make her feel special."

I nod slowly, then smile. "Everything you said makes perfect sense."

"You should be used to that by now."

I laugh.

She laughs.

I ask, "Why are you so eager to help me with this?"

"I...who knows?"

"Tell me."

"I...I just..." Her hand rises toward her face, but changes direction at the last moment and falls lightly on the highest point of the chair beside her. There's something different in her eyes. A slight sadness?

And her voice.

She only spoke a handful of words just now, but her voice was different, somehow. It had a certain depth to it. A warmth I'd never heard before.

And excuse me, but did I just witness Callie's inability to complete a simple sentence?

Something's changed. Something I can't quite wrap my brain around. It's all very mysterious, nebulous, and minute, as if a tiny shift occurred light years ago in a distant galaxy, and finally made its way to the planet Earth, into the room where Callie and I are standing.

I feel a tremor. Something stirring inside me.

Whoa, get your mind out of the gutter. I'm not talking about sex.

This is something vastly more important.

I can't take my eyes off her. "You were about to say something. Tell me."

Callie lowers her eyes. "Just that I want the best for you."

"And?"

"And I always will."

She raises her eyes and locks them on mine. "I want you to have the best possible life, Donovan."

She turns away quickly, picks up her purse—handbag—and walks to the door. She gives me one last look before leaving, and says, "I wish this for you with all my heart."

"Callie?" I say.

But she's gone.

I close my eyes, replay the scene in my head.

And it hits me.

This place, this time, this conversation. After all these years, it finally comes together for me. Hits me like a ton of bricks. Callie, my one true friend, the only person who's always been there for me—showed me a side of her she never shows, and...

And it tipped the scale. Made me realize what I've known all along, but never allowed myself to acknowledge.

I'm in love with Callie Carpenter.

It's always been there, under the surface. I've always—you know, loved her.

You know. Like a friend. And always thought of her as an amazing, unattainable sexual being. She's still that, of course. I mean, nothing's really changed regarding our relationship. Callie's still my best friend and trusted co-worker. And yes, she's an unrivaled sexual being. And she's unattainable as well, due to the fact she isn't interested in men.

So what's different?

The only thing different is what I just realized.

I love her!

I'll keep it from her, of course. Because if I ever said it in her presence, she'd howl with laughter.

And yet...I do love her.

I love Callie.

...And wish I didn't.

Chapter 41

WHEN MIRANDA AND I finally make it to Callie's condo, I do everything Callie recommended, except that when Miranda's not looking, I try to make eye contact with Callie.

But all night Callie refuses to look into my eyes.

Except once.

It happens after we finish the bottle of wine I brought to the condo a few weeks ago. We're sitting in Callie's den, and the conversation has hit a mellow stopping point.

Gwen takes advantage of the silence to ask Miranda, "When you're fucking, and Creed's on top, does it feel like old age is creeping up on you?"

Callie says, "I'm sorry, Miranda—"

But Miranda waves her off and addresses Gwen saying, "When Donovan honors me with sex, he's the only man in the world. It may sound corny to you, Gwen, but he's my treasure, and I love our time together. When my phone rings and I see it's him on the line, I feel like the luckiest woman who ever lived."

That's when Callie looks me in the eyes.

To underscore the fact Miranda defended me.

Callie says, "Miranda, I can see why Donovan is so attracted to you. You're beautiful, brilliant, classy, and everything else he bragged about when describing you to me earlier."

"Oh really?" Gwen says, her voice rising in anger. "Then why don't you fuck her!" She gets to her feet and stomps to the bedroom, and slams the door behind her.

"I should apologize for my roommate," Callie says. "She's had a bit too much to drink."

Miranda says, "Don't apologize. It can't be easy having a whore in the house. Please tell Gwen I think she's beautiful, and has a great sense of style."

Callie laughs. "You're amazing!"

"I told you Miranda was one of a kind!" I say.

Callie says, "I agree. But Miranda?"

"Yes?"

"Is there anything you'd like me to pass along to Gwen with regard to her manners?"

"Tell her I think she's funny," Miranda says. "And tell her I like her."

Callie says, "You don't have to be so sweet. Gwen's temporary."

Miranda raises an eyebrow. "You've got someone else in mind?"

Callie lowers her voice and whispers, "Dani Ripper."

"Oh, wow! You know her? Wow!"

Callie says, "We haven't met, but Dani's husband just died. We saw it on TV tonight."

Miranda says, "Seriously? God, that's tough. She's had a rough life, hasn't she?"

Callie says, "Until now, she has. But this is perfect timing! I'll put a smile on her face."

Miranda forces her own little smile, and says, "Should you give her time to grieve first?"

I say, "Callie's a pro at dating the recently widowed."

Miranda says, "There's a story here!"

Callie says, "I began dating Gwen the night her husband was murdered."

Miranda looks at me, unsure how to respond.

Callie laughs and gets to her feet. She says, "We should call it a night. Miranda, go easy on Donovan tonight. He's very fragile."

"No way!" Miranda says, laughing.

Callie says, "Donovan, she's charming."

"Thanks," I say.

Callie hugs Miranda.

I reach to hug Callie goodbye, but she takes a step back.

I give her a curious look.

She holds the door open and says, "Have a great time, both of you."

We walk out, and she closes it behind us.

On the way back to the hotel I say, "What did you think of the girls?"

"Are you asking for my general observations or a professional assessment?"

"Both."

"They're the two most beautiful women I've ever seen in the same room. Callie holds the power in their relationship. Gwen has anger issues, but Callie's anger is off the charts."

"You think?"

"If I were Gwen, I'd get the hell away from Callie, and fast. She's the sort of person who appears capable of killing without remorse."

She looks at me and says, "Oh, shit."

"What?"

"These are your friends. I'm saying bad things about them. I'm sorry."

"No, seriously. Don't hold back. I want to know."

"Callie's anger toward Gwen tells me she knows about the affair."

"What affair?"

She looks at me again. "The affair between you and Gwen."

"What?"

"I'm wrong about that?"

"No. But how did you know? Gwen made nasty comments about me all night!"

"Gwen attacks you in front of Callie to prove she's not interested in you. But those comments infuriate Callie."

"I don't see that at all."

Miranda smiles. "No, you wouldn't. But trust me. Every time Gwen looked in your direction, Callie bristled. ——Raged

"Callie's very possessive. It hurt her when Gwen cheated."

Miranda shakes her head. "It hurt her to see you and me so happy tonight, too."

"It did? Why?"

179

She laughs. "You must be the most naïve guy on the planet."

"Why?"

"Callie's in love with you."

"What? That's crazy. She likes women, not men."

"If Callie put a sign around her neck saying I Love Creed! it couldn't be more obvious."

"That doesn't make sense. She wouldn't even hug me goodbye tonight. Not to mention I've tried to put the moves on her a thousand times!"

Miranda howls with laughter. When I ask her what's so funny, she laughs harder, and laughs all the way back to the hotel.

She finally says, "Please. No more. I can't take it. My sides are hurting."

I still don't know what the hell is so funny. Or why Callie wouldn't hug me tonight.

Chapter 42

"WE'RE GOING GAMBLING?" Miranda says. "At this hour?"

It's early morning. Although Bob Koltech is waiting at General Aviation to fly us to Highland, Illinois, I suddenly ask the limo driver to swing by Caesers Palace for a few minutes, causing Miranda to wonder if I've been hit by the gambling bug.

I hold up my phone and say, "I just got a text message from Kimberly. She and her boyfriend broke up last night, and she spent the night at Caesers."

"Well, she's young," Miranda says. "They'll probably be back in each others' arms by midnight."

"I hope not."

She arches an eyebrow. "You don't approve?"

I smile. Miranda couldn't, and shouldn't know that Kimberly killed her boyfriend last night. She might jump to the conclusion we have a dysfunctional family.

"I like the kid just fine," I say. "I don't approve of his job."

She smiles. "The kid?"

"Chuck."

"And what's Chuck's job?"

"He's a pre-rapture pet salesman."

Miranda laughs.

"What?"

"I don't approve of the kid, either!" she says.

We get to Caesers and I go up to Kimberly's room alone.

First thing she says is, "Are you going to give me a lecture?"

"Of course not."

"Really, Father?"

"Well, a short one."

She sighs, and motions me to enter her hotel room.

"I have a major history with Sam Case," I say. "That's how he found and targeted you."

"I know. Sam told me everything before he died."

"By everything, you mean?"

"He said you stole his wife and ruined his business. Is that true?"

I try to think of a nicer way to put it, but I think she's already put it the nicest way possible.

"I'll take your silence as a yes," she says.

"I ruined his business," I said, "but his business was illegal."

"Oh, please."

I shrug.

"And the wife? Can I assume she forced herself on you?"

"Not at first," I say. "But regardless, he had no right to punish me by manipulating you into becoming a killer."

"Sam didn't do that."

"What do you mean?"

"Sam only found me a few weeks ago. Some other guy started the whole gain-my-trust-and-turn-me-into-a-killer thing. Then he turned it over to Sam."

"What other guy?"

"Sam called him Darwin." She looks at me. "Are you okay?"

I nod.

"So what's the lecture part?" she says. "I should've called you first?"

"No. I understand why you didn't."

"Then what's the lecture about?"

"Sam stole my identity. Probably had a broader plan to clean out my bank accounts some day. But anyway, he checked into the hotel under my name. Which means—"

"Shit. I killed him in your hotel room and walked away." She frowns. "I suck at this."

"No. You're amazing at this. You just need some training."

She looks up at me. "So...I can still work with you?"

"For me. Not with me."

She smiles.

I say, "Are you okay?"

"You're asking because of the way I cut him up?"

"Yup."

"I never used a knife before. The knife made it so...uh..." She's searching for the word. I provide it.

"Personal."

"Yes, exactly! The knife made it so personal. It was hard, cutting through the tendons, and when all that stringy stuff scraped and clicked, it was completely unexpected."

"Maybe we'll ask Santa to get you a sharper knife."

"Good, 'cause it took forever to saw through the muscle fibers. And who'd have known how much blood would spurt? And how far?"

"You knew, because you didn't get it on your clothes."

"Right. But still, it was really gruesome."

"And?"

"I keep reliving it, over and over, in my mind. The look of terror on his face. The helplessness in his eyes."

"And?"

"And every time I re-live it, I feel better about what I did to him."

"That's what we call a good kill, honey."

"Thank you, Daddy."

Chapter 43

WE'RE ON THE jet now, wheels up. Maybe's going to spend some time with Callie this afternoon, so we can get a better handle on how competent she is and how much she needs to learn. I suspect Darwin helped her obtain the physical skills and emotional mindset necessary to kill people, but she's obviously got a lot to learn about the technical aspects of the business.

The good news is she's young, and eager to learn.

The better news is she's got Callie as a trainer.

The best news is she's a natural.

I'd go on and on about it, but Sal's calling me.

When I answer he says, "You're not gonna believe this shit!"

"Tell me."

"You know my niece?"

"Which one?"

"Sophie Alexander."

"No."

"Yeah you do. You met her at my birthday party. When you were with—whatcha call—"

"Kathleen."

"Whatever. Okay, so you don't remember, no problem. Anyway, I got this niece—"

"Sophie Alexander."

"Right, and she's a singer and songwriter."

"Wait," I say. "I remember her. Cute brunette. Big hair, sweet voice."

"That's her!" he says.

"What about her?"

"She's gonna be—whatcha call—performing at my Fourth of July party."

"That should make you very happy. And proud."

"Yeah, whatever. So, are you coming?"

"I'm still working it out."

"Reason I ask," he says, then pauses for effect.

"Yes?"

He laughs. "You haven't seen the news!"

"What news?"

"You're gonna love this!"

"How good could it possibly be?"

"Oh, it's good," he says.

"Sal. I'm 42,000 feet in the sky, on a jet. Tell me your big news before we lose reception."

"You remember Dani Ripper?"

"How could I not? The whole country's talking about her."

"She's been staying with someone since the story broke."

"Right. So what?"

"Guess who she's been staying with?"

"The Blues Magoos? Lord Fauntleroy? A family of polar bears?"

"My niece, Sophie Alexander."

"You're shitting me!"

He laughs again. "I told you you'd love it!"

"I do. When can I meet them?"

"At my Fourth of July party!"

"That's in what, five weeks?"

"Not soon enough? I can get you into her husband's funeral, if you want."

"When's that?"

"Friday."

"You're going?"

"Fuck no! Are you crazy? Her husband drops dead in Cincinnati where I live and work? And Dani happens to be staying with my niece? You think they might wonder why I'm at the funeral?"

"You're going to need my help."

"With what?"

"When the cops make the connection they'll arrest Dani for the murder. Then they'll come looking for you."

"Me? What the fuck?"

"Guilt by association. They'll put the screws to Dani and Sophie and find out what happened."

"Nothing happened."

"Right. Here's my question. Can you trust the shooter? Or do I need to get involved."

"There is no fuckin' shooter! Sophie says the guy died of a heart attack."

"Sal."

"Yeah?"

"I saw the husband on TV."

"So?"

"No way he died of a heart attack."

"I had nothing to do with it. Hell, I didn't even know they were a couple till today."

"Who's a couple?"

"Dani and Sophie."

"Holy shit!" I say.

"I know. We were hoping Sophie would marry a rich country singer."

"This is great news!"

"What? Why?"

"Callie will be thrilled."

"Why?"

"Because—" I stop. I can't tell him Callie might steal his niece's girlfriend. Nor can I tell him I'm excited to learn Dani likes women because maybe Callie and I will have a chance to hook up if Gwen's not at the party. But Sal lets it slide. He only cares about one thing.

"You think Callie will come to my party?"

"I can guarantee it."

"Tell her to wear a—whatcha call—bikini."

"I will. But Sal?"

"Yeah?"

"I'll need to get involved in the investigation. They're not going to let this slide. Dani's as high profile as it gets. This has to be handled properly."

"Why are you saying this to me? I told you I didn't do it."

188

"What about Sophie?"

"What about her?"

"With the husband dead, she has a clear path to Dani."

"If she wanted the husband killed, she'd go through me."

"And she didn't."

"That's what I'm saying."

"Okay. So who's got her now?"

"Dani?"

"Yeah."

"Nashville P.D."

"You know anyone in the department?"

"Are you kidding me?"

"I'll take that as a yes."

"What do you need?" Sal says.

"Find out who's got the case, and what they know."

"What're you gonna do?"

"Put a plan together."

"When?"

"It's Tuesday, funeral's Friday. The cops will be all over Dani between now and then. But starting Monday, it's going to get ugly."

"Why?"

"By then the FBI will have the case. I'll have to short-circuit their investigation Monday."

"Shit," Sal says.

"What's wrong?"

"I don't have any contacts among the feds. Do you?"

"One."

"Who?"

"Their boss."

"Who's their boss," Sal says. "Congress?"

"The president."

"You know the fuckin' president well enough to shut down the investigation?"

"No. But by Monday I will."

"Why's that?"

"By Monday—and probably much sooner—he's going to owe me, big time."

Chapter 44

HIGHLAND-WINET AIRPORT is four miles north-west of Highland, Illinois, and less than five minutes from the home of Miles Gundy. We land, and I sign for the rental car. Within minutes I'm turning right on Atlantic Avenue.

"Gundy's house?" Miranda says.

"Yup."

"Lou said it might be booby trapped."

"That's why you're going to wait in the car."

When I turn into the driveway she says, "This is how you do it?"

"What?"

"Don't you park somewhere and scope out the scene first? Get a feel for what's happening?"

I notice she's got her compact out, checking her makeup.

"I probably should scope out the scene, but I don't watch as much TV as you."

"You're making fun of me."

"A little."

"So you're just going to what, find an open window in the back? Pick a lock?"

"People don't leave their windows unlocked in real life. And while I can certainly pick a lock, it's easier to kick the door in."

"Won't that make a lot of noise?"

"Yup."

"You're not concerned about the neighbors?"

"Nope."

"Why not?"

"I make neighbors nervous."

"They'll call the police."

"I doubt that. But if they do, I'll handle it."

"How?"

"Miranda?"

"Yes, honey?"

"This is what I do. Can you just sit back, finish powdering your nose, and let me do it? I mean, no offense, but I could've been inside by now."

"Just tell me how you'd handle the police."

I take a deep breath and let it out slowly.

"If it's not too much trouble," she adds, sweetly.

"If the cops show up I'll say I came to check on Miles because I haven't heard from him in days. When he didn't answer the door, I kicked it in, concerned he might have suffered a heart attack. He has a heart condition, you see, and I'm his cardiologist."

"You are?"

"I've got papers to prove it."

"Cool."

"You're happy now?" I say.

"Yes. Thank you."

"Anything else?"

"Nope. Off you go!"

I open the door and start to get out, but stop long enough to ask, "Just out of curiosity, why are you so worried about the cops?

"Because there are two policemen in the car behind us, watching the house."

I frown, and look in the mirror. Must be the angle, but I don't see them. I climb out of the car and as I turn to look, an unmarked police car turns into the driveway and comes to a stop two feet behind my rental car.

They exit the vehicle and tell me to put my hands where they can see them. One approaches, one stays back.

"Are you Miles Gundy?"

"No, but I hope to catch him at home."

"Why?"

"Follow up interview."

"For what?"

"I'm a corporate recruiter."

"A what?"

"Some folks say headhunter."

"Like in Africa?"

"You're kidding, right?" I pause. "No? Well anyway, I hire unemployed executives. Mr. Gundy's a chemist, looking for work. I've got a possible job for him."

"You got an ID?"

I show him one.

"Donovan Creed?"

"That's right."

"And who's this with you?" he says, pointing at my passenger.

"Miranda Rodriguez, director of Human Resources, NYU."

He walks around to the passenger side, taps on the window. She looks up.

"Can you step out of the car, Miss?"

He stands back while she opens the door.

"ID, please?"

She shows him her driver's license.

"You're a long way from New York."

"So are you," she says.

"Gundy's not here," the cop says. "But we're looking for him."

"Can I ask why?" Miranda says.

"You can ask. Doesn't mean I'll answer."

"Well, if he's done something wrong, I'd like to know about it. We're looking to employ an honest chemist, not a law-breaker."

The other cop likes the way Miranda fits her jeans. He walks over and says, "His prior employer reported some dangerous chemicals have gone missing. We're waiting for him to show up, see if he knows anything about that."

"His prior employer?" Miranda says. "Esson Pharmaceuticals, of St. Louis?"

He consults his notes. "Yes, ma'am. Gundy's supervisor, Ephram Livingston, reported the property stolen.

"Dr. Livingston, I presume?" Miranda says, without the slightest hint of a smile.

He consults his notes furiously before giving up. "I'll have to assume he's a doctor," he says. "Strange name, though, don't you think? Ephram?"

"My father's name was Ephram," she says, shamelessly. "He died in a car crash, when I was a child."

"I'm so sorry!" he says. Then adds, "I certainly didn't mean to imply I don't like the name. It's a fine name. Just unusual, is all."

Miranda smiles. "You've done me a kindness, informing me about the reported theft. That was very gallant of you."

"Gallant," the first cop says.

"How so?" the second cop says, trying to sound sophisticated.

"We've narrowed our job search to two applicants. Mr. Gundy, and Ms. Possumdegumstump."

She looks at me and says, "Mr. Creed, I think we can safely say Ms. Possumdegumstump is our new head chemist."

"Swell," I say.

The second cop tips his hat.

"Glad to be of service," he says. "Will you be staying in our fair city overnight?"

"Our fair city?" the first cop sneers.

"Alas, no," Miranda says. "Our winning candidate lives in St. Louis. I suppose we'll be heading there now."

She looks at me. "Is that correct, Mr. Creed?"

I nod.

"Oh, pooh!" she says.

"Well, until next time," he says.

"Until then," she says.

As we get back in the car we hear the first cop say "Oh, poo!" to his partner.

I wait for them to back out of the driveway. When they do, I follow suit, and Miranda waves to the cops as I head down the street.

"Ms. Possumdegumstump?" I say.

She smiles. "That's right."

"Because?"

"In my experience, a longer, stranger name is more believable than a common one, like Smith or Jones."

"I'll say it again. Come work for me."

"No."

"I'll pay you three thousand dollars a week."

"That's very generous, but no."

I sigh. "You're a heartbreaker."

"Good thing you're a cardiologist."

"Thirty-five hundred."

"No."

I turn right at the intersection, left on Fairway.

"Where to, Mr. Headhunter?"

"We'll go ahead and pick up Miles."

"You know where he is?"

"I do."

"You're joking, right?"

"Nope."

"If you knew where he was, why did you want to kick in his door?"

"Evidence."

"Ah."

Chapter 45

"LOOK FOR TWELVE-forty-two," I say, as we turn onto Vincent.

"You think he's staying with his ex and her sister?"

"No, I think he's stalking them."

"You're going to capture him, right? Then torture him?"

"Yes. You still want to be a part of it?"

"Yes."

"You might want to re-think that."

"Why?"

"I'm going to take my time," I say. "He's going to suffer."

"I'll watch as much as I can. But mostly I want to talk to him."

"Then you shall. Okay, it should be somewhere on this block."

"There's twelve-twenty-eight," Miranda says. "Slow down, it's...okay, it's two houses up, on the right."

"The gray ranch? Red shutters?"

"Yes."

"Keep your eyes peeled for a white Honda Accord."

"Okay," she says. "If we see one, I've got the license number in my purse."

"You mean your handbag?" I say, trying to sound hip.

"Actually, I was referring to my coin purse."

"The one you keep inside your hand bag?"

She gives me a strange look. "Where else would I keep it?"

I drive to the intersection, turn right, make the block.

No white Honda Accord.

This time when I pass the house I go two blocks.

"Bingo!" I say.

"Where?"

"Next block, left side."

She digs in her handbag for her coin purse, opens it, and removes the notes she took back in Virginia.

"4XT167C," she says.

I pass the car.

"Guy in the driver's seat," I say.

Miranda checks the license plate against her notes.

"Omigod!" she says. "It's him!"

I drive another block, make a u-turn, and find a place to park where I can keep an eye on Miles.

"What happens next?" she says.

"We watch and wait."

"How long?"

"Until he moves or it gets dark."

"Donovan?"

"Yeah?"

"I need to use the bathroom."

"You're kidding."

"Nope."

"How long can you hold it?"

"Umm...ten, maybe fifteen minutes?"

I sigh. It's three-fifteen, broad daylight. We're in a residential area.

I reach across her, open the glove compartment, and pop the trunk.

"Hang on a second," I say.

I get out of the car and remove my duffel from the trunk. Then come around to her side and open her door.

"What's up?"

"You're going to drive."

"Where?"

"I'm going to walk along the sidewalk toward his car. When I get there, I need you to drive right up beside him, lower the passenger window, and ask him where the nearest fast food restaurant is."

"Then what?"

"Try to engage him in conversation."

"Then what?"

"Then drive to the fast food place and pee. Then drive back here and park the car. If you don't see me, call my cell phone."

"What if he drives away while I'm gone?"

"We'll follow him."

She says, "You're going to put a tracking device on his car while I'm engaging him in conversation."

"Thirty-eight hundred a week. That's my final offer."

She giggles. "Sorry, no."

I shake my head. "I'll talk you into it, eventually."

"I don't think so."

As I walk down the sidewalk toward Gundy's car, Lou Kelly calls to tell me two dozen kids and three adults were poisoned at a birthday party in Nashville two days ago.

"Sunday? Same day as the Derby City Fair?"

"Same day. One of the moms gave a description. Said a guy showed up at the party with a cookie cake, and there was something odd about him."

"Odd how?"

"The way he stared at her gave her the creeps, so she followed him through the house and out the front door, and saw him drive away in a white Honda Accord."

"The three adults?" I say.

"All Moms."

"Damn it, Lou! Why did it take you two days to make the connection?"

"I just found out about it this minute."

"How's that possible?"

"The cookie cake was laced with ricin."

Ricin poison takes two to four days to kill, depending on the age and health of the victim.

"They must've all gotten sick the same day. Why didn't anyone report it?"

"It was a kids' birthday party. The moms figured the kids ate too much, or maybe the potato salad was bad. They started calling each other last night to compare notes, but still didn't want to offend the hosts."

"But all that changed today?"

"Right."

"How bad is it, Lou?"

"The kids are all dying or dead. The moms will probably survive."

I'm closing in on Miles's car.

"Son of a bitch!" I say.

Looking behind me, I see Miranda pulling out into the road. I press her number on my cell phone.

"Is this too soon?" she says.

"When you pull next to him, keep six feet of distance between the cars."

"Okay."

She passes me and pulls up alongside him, keeping a six-foot distance between their windows.

I'm directly behind his car now.

Miles is staring ahead so intently he hasn't noticed Miranda's car yet.

She taps her horn.

He looks up.

She motions him to lower his window.

He does.

She says, "I'm sorry to bother you, but can you tell me if there's a fast food restaurant nearby?"

At that point I walk between the two cars, pull my .357 Magnum from my duffel, and blow his fucking head off.

Miranda screams.

I open the passenger door, climb in, and she speeds off down the street.

"Omigod! Omigod! Omigod!" she screams.

"Sorry," I say. "Change of plans."

"Omigod!" she screams again. "That was fantastic!"

"It was?"

"Omigod! I loved it!"

"Ten thousand dollars a week," I say.

"Done!" she says.

Chapter 46

WHAT? HOLY SHIT, I don't believe it! You're here with us on the private jet?

Seriously, I don't believe it.

Look, can you give us a few minutes of privacy?

Miranda and I are having sex.

No, I'm not giving details. Except that she's "Totally into it!"

Her words, not mine.

So please. Show some class. Give me a few minutes here.

Chapter 47

THANKS. I needed that.

Chapter 48

MIRANDA AND I touch down in Santa Monica, California. I've reserved a suite in the same location on the beach where I stayed nearly four years ago. It's a beautiful hotel, brand new, what they call a boutique hotel.

The old hotel got blown up while I was in it! I found out about the bomb just before it detonated. I actually had to jump off the second floor balcony to escape.

You may have read about it.

My future associate, Miranda, loves the place. Although she agreed to work for me, she refuses to start until next June, a year from now.

Why?

She wants to finish school, then travel to Europe for several months with her friend.

No, not a guy.

Her girl friend.

No, not a female lover.

A friend.

Yes, I'm certain, because I asked her the same questions. I also spent two hours trying to talk her out of going. Then I spent an hour trying to talk her into letting me come with her instead of her friend.

But no.

"At least let me visit you in Europe," I asked. "We'll have dinner."

"No," she said. "I'm already giving up my dream of running my own practice to work for you. And don't think for a minute I don't know how you operate!"

"What's that supposed to mean?"

"It means working for you won't be a nine to five job. It'll be an all-hours-of-the-night job, and one that will ruin any chance I have of living a normal life. I've worked my ass off to get these degrees, and I'm not going to jump into a twenty-four-seven job until I've done something fun for myself."

"You'd rather be with your friend than me?"

"Yes. Absolutely."

"   W   h   y   ?   "

"Donovan, you sound like a ten-year-old."

"You've always encouraged me to express my feelings."

"Look, I love being with you, and hope you'll let me give you the best two days of your life, starting right now. But if you bring this up one more time, I'm going to book the next flight back to New York, and I'll never work for you."

"Okay. Sorry. You know about my abandonment issues."

"I do."

I sigh. "I'm happy for you."

"Thank you."

"I'm jealous, though."

"I know."

The two days went by as fast as perfect days always do. I won't tell you how many times we laughed, or made love, or what we talked about, or how many drinks we had. I will say the hotel lounge has a wonderful house band, and Miranda shocked me by getting up on stage and singing a beautiful song called Someone Like You, by someone named Adele.

What shocked me was how amazing Miranda's voice is! I mean, I've never heard anyone sing like that! Her voice was powerful when power was needed, but tender and haunting the rest of the time.

I'm serious, she was spectacular!

By the time she finished her song, everyone in the room was on their feet, cheering, with tears streaming down their faces! If Adele's version is half as good as Miranda's, well, she'll probably have a hit on her hands.

On Friday, Sal calls with the news about Dani Ripper's interrogation.

"The lead detective's a guy named Marco Polomo."

"Is he from Cincinnati or Nashville?"

"Nashville. They interrogated her on Tuesday."

"I saw on TV where she's back at your niece's house."

"Right. There's a million cops and reporters surrounding the place. Cops are actually living inside the friggin' house."

"Today's the funeral?"

"It was this morning. They're probably back in Nashville by now."

"What's Polomo saying?"

"He's one of my guys on the inside. He's managed to keep Sophie out of it, but like you guessed, the FBI's coming in on Monday."

"Do they know who's investigating?"

"Guy named Agent Chase. They don't know his first name, but Polomo's shitting his pants because I told him I want Dani cleared and he says there's nothing he can do at this point."

"Why not?"

"Apparently the Cincinnati police have found a bunch of evidence that—whatcha call—implicates Dani. And Polomo's concerned if they get Dani, they'll find a way to pull Sophie into it because of her police record."

"Sophie's got a police record?"

"Sort of. It's been—whatcha call—expunged, but it's still there for those who know how to look."

"What did she do?"

"She, you know, fell in with the wrong crowd. It's not important. She's a good girl. I don't want to talk about it."

"Okay."

"Okay what?"

"Okay, I'll take care of it."

"You'll talk to the president?"

"I'll get him the message."

"What if he won't play ball?"

"He'll play."

"You got something on him?"

"Nope."

"Then how do you know he'll cooperate?"

"He fears me."

"Smart man, our president. I always said so."
"You like him?"
"I voted for him twelve times. So did all my people."
"Twelve times?"
"In the same election."

Chapter 49

"THEY'RE STILL CHECKING Gundy's house," Lou says, "and they're going to pin the Derby City Fair attack on him, but they're not going to declare him responsible for poisoning the kids in Nashville."

"Why not?"

"The official explanation?"

"Go ahead."

"They don't have enough evidence."

"What's the real reason?"

"My opinion?"

"Yeah."

"I think the administration doesn't want to admit they failed to issue a warning when you made the recommendation."

"And why didn't they?"

"They thought it would create a panic situation. Plus, they weren't convinced one guy did it, or that he'd do it again."

"Technically they were right. He didn't put poison in any other dispensers, as far as we know."

"No. But he did something far worse with the ricin. And you know the media culture we're dealing with today, right?"

"Yeah. No matter who you are, or what you've done, or how many people you've helped, or what you've stood for all your life, the only thing that counts is if you could have done more. If they can make a case you could have done more, you're toast."

"And the president doesn't want to be toast," Lou says.

"Which is why he's going to work with me on this Dani Ripper thing."

"Do you really want me to go so far as to threaten the president?"

"No. I want you to tell Sherm Phillips I'm threatening the president."

"What's the threat, specifically?"

"You're taping me."

He pauses. "Yes."

"The specific threat is the president could have done more. I warned him this guy was going to keep attacking. I happen to know Dani and Sophie are innocent, and I like having Sal Bonadello owing me a huge favor."

"Donovan?"

"Yeah?"

"You sort of rambled there. What's the specific threat you're making?"

"I'll tell the media the president could have done more."

"And if he says it's your word against his?"

"I'll explain how we found the guy, and how we know he killed those children at the birthday party in Nashville. And you know what's really scary?"

"What's that?"

"I bet Gundy did some other shit we don't even know about yet. Which means the president can still do more."

"Got it. I'll let you know what he says."

To my surprise, I get my answer forty minutes later.

"Sherm says this thing with Dani and Sophie is going to be on your ass."

"Okay."

"I'm serious, Donovan. If it turns out you're wrong, and one or both of them killed Dani's husband, they're going to sell you out."

"I can live with that. So how's it going down?"

"You'll meet with Agent Chase on Sunday. He'll show you the evidence. He's hard core, meaning, he's not going to drop the case without interviewing the girl."

"But?"

"But you'll go with him to Sophie's house for the interview. You'll watch how Dani handles the questions. If you're convinced she's innocent, you'll make the call. He'll abide by your decision."

"He's okay with me impersonating an FBI agent?"

"He is not. But the president okayed it."

"Personally?"

"No, of course not. But yes, through Sherm. So how does all this sound to you?"

"Perfect, for two reasons. First, I get to meet Dani in person. Second, I get to spend two more days with Miranda."

"Good for you."

"Speaking of good things, I'm very happy for your promotion."

"I only got it because you didn't want it."

"That's not true. You're a diplomat. They respect that."

"I suspect Holden Prescott didn't want me, but he must have been outvoted. It helped that I took all the credit for you catching and killing Miles Gundy."

"I couldn't have done it without you and the geeks. So, do you have a code name yet?"

"They decided against the whole code name dynamic. None of them knew for sure who Darwin was. They don't want to make the same mistake twice."

"Well, either way, I'm proud to work for you, Lou. You'll be a helluva better boss than Darwin."

He laughs. "Work for me? You've never worked for anyone in your life! You'll only do the things you agree with. We both know that. The difference between me and Darwin is I know not to expect anything else."

"See what I mean? You're already better at this than Darwin."

Chapter 50

AGENT CHASE DOESN'T like me.

Ask me if I give a shit.

Look at him leering at me. He's as big and powerful as a horse, and as fit as you can get outside of prison. He's also really steamed, which would work against him in a fight.

He's sizing me up, convinced he can take me.

But he's wrong.

He's a rough, tough, no-nonsense guy, but there are different ways to measure tough. He tests his against recruits. I test mine against the military's latest torture weapons. Over four years I've built up my stamina against the ADS weapon. The one they banned citing it cruel and inhumane. See, the army's only allowed to use humane weapons in combat situations these days. I can handle twenty-two seconds of constant exposure to the ADS weapon. Second best in the world is three seconds. You think the difference of nineteen seconds is a small one? Let me put it in perspective. The three-second guy would kick Agent Chase's ass.

Don't fuck with me, Agent Chase. I don't play fair.

I've read up on Agent Chase these past two days, and asked around. He's got a reputation as a fierce fighter, with years of hand-to-hand combat training under his ninth-degree black belt. Maybe before this is over he'll try to show me how tough he is.

Agent Chase is a hard-working, honest man, and the world is better off for having people like him in it. I respect him, and that's the truth. But he needs to sit there and deal with it, because this thing with Dani and Sophie has already been decided.

It's political.

You hate politics, don't you, Agent Chase?

Me too.

But while this is politics, I happen to be on the right side. You're convinced Dani and Sophie are guilty, but you're wrong. For you to be right, Sal Bonadello has to be wrong.

And Sal isn't wrong.

You have a greater respect for evidence than Sal does. Maybe it's because you never planted evidence.

Sal has. In fact, he's a master of planting evidence. And he says the evidence against Ben and Dani was planted, but not by his niece or Dani.

And I believe him.

So deal with it.

This is as good a time as any to stop giving me your evil game-face stare. It means nothing to me. While I respect the hell out of you, I'm not going to hold back if you come at me.

You and I are like Ernest Hemingway and Jack Dempsey. Jack always refused to box exhibitions with Ernest Hemingway because Hemingway was a big guy with a lot of training. In other words, in his world, he could fight. He had just enough training to be dangerous. When a man is dangerous, a guy like Dempsey can't take the time to pull his punches.

Jack didn't refuse to fight Hemingway because he feared him.

He refused to fight him because he respected him, and didn't want to hurt, or possibly kill him.

That's how I feel about Agent Chase.

These gym boxers and self-defense experts think they can handle themselves because they've kicked ass all their lives in the real world. But the real world isn't Jack Dempsey's world of elite fighters, and it's not my world. I kill killers and terrorists, not angry civilians and bank robbers. The people I fight don't come at you the way they do in the FBI handbook.

Agent Chase needs to cool the fuck down. Because there's always a moment of truth when these hard asses learn what kill or be killed really means. It means when the attack gets out of hand there's no one in the room blowing a whistle to end the carnage.

I speak to him respectfully. I go so far as to tell him I respect him.

That seems to help. He's not happy, but he's talking. Maybe we'll be friends before this is over. Wait, he's about to say something warm and fuzzy.

"You respect me?" he says. "I'm one of the good guys. I don't need your respect. And don't kid yourself we're going to be friends when this is over. I've asked around. I know all about you. I want it on the record between us that I don't approve of you or what you stand for. It's people like you who weaken the moral fiber of our country."

"Is your office in downtown Cincinnati?" I ask.

"Yeah. So what?"

I decide he knows nothing about me. I could explain how I saved his life by preventing downtown Cincinnati from being wiped off the face of the earth a few years back, but that information is classified beyond his pay grade.

"Were you making a threat just now, Mr. Creed?"

I sigh. He's trying to goad me, calling me "mister" to prove I don't have a title.

"Let's just move along," I say, "and I'll stay out of your life as best I can."

"That would be wise," he says.

He tells me how the meeting with Dani Ripper is going to go down tomorrow.

We work out a signal. After the interview is concluded, if I'm still satisfied Dani's innocent, I'll put my hands together and form a steeple with my index fingers.

I demonstrate it, and he nods.

Chapter 51

I'M NOT GOING to hit you with a bunch of details about the Dani Ripper back story and investigation. It's fascinating, but that could take up a whole book.

Maybe Dani will write one someday.

For now, here's what you need to know: Dani's husband died in their home in Cincinnati last week while the house was surrounded by reporters. Dani was staying with her friend, Sophie, in Nashville, at the time. Everyone agrees Ben died of natural causes, but the evidence found at his home "proves" he raped and killed a local minor, Jaqui Moreland. Jaqui's death has become a thorn in the side of local law enforcement. You know the drill, everyone's hot to solve the case. If Ben is good for Jaqui's murder, the city goes back to being a safe place to live and raise children.

It's to everyone's advantage that Ben killed Jaqui Moreland.

Except that Dani Ripper doesn't believe it. She thinks Ben has been murdered and framed for the killing. She's a private eye, and had been personally investigating Jaqui's death. Had even been hired by Jaqui's mother at one point, to help find her missing daughter.

Agent Chase thinks Dani knows more than she's saying. He believes Dani knew her husband was a murderer, and may have been covering up for him.

Here's Dani's problem. If she's right, and Ben was murdered and framed for raping and killing the little girl, she and Sophie become the prime suspects. Sophie has mob connections for the killing, and Dani had access to the house for planting the evidence.

Tomorrow morning Agent Chase is going to grill the beautiful and vulnerable Dani Ripper. He's going to show her some gruesome crime scene photos and evidence, and I need to decide if her reaction to them is authentic.

In other words, did she know her husband was a murderer? Has she seen these pictures before? After judging her reaction, if I honestly believe she's innocent, I have the power to shut down the investigation.

But what if I think she's lying? What then?

Simple.

I'll let Agent Chase do his job, and I'll deal with Sal on my own.

Chapter 52

SOPHIE'S HOUSE IS upper-middle class, simple, but tasteful. But the furnishings and paintings are exquisite. There's money here, and I don't think it came from writing songs, as everyone claims. I mean, some of it did. She's written several highly-successful country hits. But you know how I am. There's cash hidden in a painting somewhere in this house, or maybe a stash of crystal meth in one of the walls.

I can feel it.

What gives me that impression? Sophie had a criminal record at one time, that's so bad Sal doesn't even want to discuss it. Also, when I suggested Sophie might have hired someone to kill Dani's husband, Sal said, "If she wanted the husband killed, she'd go through me."

Which is very different than if he'd said, "Sophie knows nothing about such things."

Sophie and Dani are in the kitchen when I enter the house with Agent Chase and Nashville police detective Marco

Polomo. Polomo introduces us, and the first thing I notice is Dani could be Callie's younger sister. The resemblance is remarkable.

Dani's polite, and has an All-American Girl look about her. Sophie's quite pretty in her own right, maybe five years older, and appears to be much more worldly.

Polomo asks Sophie to leave the room, but Dani says, "You may as well let Sophie stay, because first, it's her house, and second, I'm going to tell her everything the minute you leave."

Polomo gives in. "Where can we sit and talk?"

"My attorney just called. He's on his way."

"Figures," I say, trying to play my part of the big, bad FBI agent.

Polomo winks at me when no one's looking. He knows I'm there to help. While Dani, Chase, and Polomo make small talk in the den, Sophie catches my eye and leaves the room. I follow her into her bedroom.

She whispers, "They're letting you impersonate an FBI agent?"

"Yup."

"Can you really get this thing shut down?"

"If I believe she's innocent."

"She is. I guarantee it."

"I hope you're right."

"I don't like Agent Chase," she says.

"He's just trying to do his job."

"Is he going to go after her really hard?"

"Yes."

"I have a temper. It's gotten me into trouble before."

"Tell you what, if Agent Chase says something that sets you off?"

"Yeah?"

"Smack him."

"What?"

"Slap the shit out of him."

"He's a federal officer."

"I know. Isn't it great?"

"If I hit him, you'll protect me?"

"I will. And I'll tell Sal. And he'll laugh his ass off."

Sophie smiles. "I like you. And not just because you're handsome."

"Thanks."

Dani's lawyer, Chris Fist, shows up. We join the others in the den and Agent Chase opens a manila envelope and places a photograph on the coffee table in front of Dani.

"Recognize this?" he says.

Chris says, "You can answer the question honestly."

Dani answers, "No."

"No you don't recognize it?"

"I don't. Nor do I have any idea what it is," she says.

"It's a voice altering device."

"Like the kind Roy used when he left that message?"

"Yes. Except this one was found in your home."

"My home? Where?"

"Ben's desk drawer."

He pulls out another photo and sets it in front of her. It's a picture of a hand-made box. "Ever seen this?" Chase says.

"No, but it's gorgeous."

"It was found in your basement, in a cardboard box, under a pile of old college essays and lesson plans."

"When?"

"The day you authorized the Cincinnati police to conduct a thorough search of your home."

"That was a week ago! Why are you just now showing me this?"

"What difference does it make?" he says. "You've either seen it or you haven't."

"She hasn't," Chris Fist says.

"It took us two days to find the key," Agent Chase says.

"Okay."

"Know where we found it?"

Chris says, "If she's never seen the box, how would she know where you found the key? Assuming there's a point to these questions, can you get to it?"

Agent Chase says, "You know the small, framed photo of you on Ben's desk, to the left of his computer? You're younger, big smile, wearing a yellow blouse. There's a horse fence and a tree in the background."

Dani takes a minute to dab the tears from her eyes, thinking about it.

"I know the picture," she says. "It was Ben's favorite."

"The key was hidden between the photo and the backing, between two pieces of cardboard."

Sophie says, "What's in the box?"

Chase says, "Glad you asked."

He pulls three photos from the manila envelope and spreads them out in front of Dani.

It takes her a moment to realize what she's seeing.

Then she starts screaming, and Sophie' hand flies across the coffee table and connects against the side of Agent Chase's face so hard it knocks him back.

Sophie isn't just having fun. She's genuinely angry. I think she would've hit him even if I hadn't given her permission.

"What the fuck's the matter with you?" she screams, and cocks her arm to slap me.

Me? She really is pissed!

But Chris Fist lunges and manages to restrain her.

"Your client just assaulted a federal agent!" Chase yells, rubbing the side of his face.

"Fuck you!" Sophie says, trying to squirm out of Chris's grip.

"I could have you arrested for this!" Chase yells. "Tell her, Mr. Fist."

Chris says, "First of all, Sophie's not my client. Second, she asked you a fair question. Why the hell would you ambush Dani with these photos? You think she hasn't been through enough in her twenty-four years?"

"Watch your tone, counselor."

"Watch yours, you piece of shit."

Polomo and I exchange a glance. Our facial expressions show we're horrified by these developments. But we're laughing like hell on the inside.

Sophie says, "Dani?

Dani can't stop looking at the photos. The two that count are first, a photo of blood-stained panties, and second, Jaqui Moreland, naked and duct-taped, eyes wide with terror.

Agent Chase says, "The photo's authentic. This is Jaqui Moreland, moments before her death. We're still waiting on the DNA results, but the panties match the description in her mother's original statement. By the way, we never disclosed Jaqui's panties were absent the crime scene."

"Put the photos away," Chris says.

Agent Chase says, "We've spent the past week trying to decide if you had any knowledge your husband raped and killed Jaqui Moreland."

"What?"

"Maybe ManChild set him up," she says.

ManChild being the name the media gave Jaqui's killer.

Chase says, "We lifted Ben's fingerprints off the photograph. The threatening call you received was made with a voice-altering device exactly like the one in Ben's home office."

"Why would Ben try to frighten me?" she says. "I knew nothing about it. I've spent endless time and money trying to catch ManChild. Everyone knows that."

"Which is exactly what made us suspicious," Agent Chase says. "If you're trying to protect Ben Davis, what better cover could you possibly have than to act like you're spending every waking hour searching for Jaqui's killer?"

Chris Fist says, "Do you have anything to charge her with, or were you just trying to get her reaction to the photos?"

Chase looks at my hands and sees I've made them into a steeple.

He says, "We were testing her reaction."

"And?"

"My professional opinion? She's either completely innocent," he pauses and looks me in the eyes. "Or one hell of an actress."

By late afternoon all the phone calls are made to those who need to hear that Agent Chase and the FBI have officially cleared Dani Ripper of any involvement in her husband's death, planting evidence, or having prior knowledge of his guilt. Chase agrees to call Chris Fist in the morning, so he can give Dani the good news.

I reach to shake his hand.

He declines.

Chapter 53

Miranda Rodriguez.

MIRANDA LOVES SPENDING time with Donovan Creed. After seeing how he lives, the idea of private practice seemed incredibly boring. She knew from the first day she wanted to work for him, but one thing about Miranda, she's always been a shrewd negotiator. So she kept saying no. When the salary offer became astronomical, she finally relented, then gave him something else to worry about. Like not starting for a year.

Saying goodbye was the hardest part. She made him promise not to call or see her for a full year.

Will he keep his promise?

She hopes so, because immediately moving in with Rose is a vital part of the contract she signed with her friend. She'll finish the semester, as planned, and get her master's degree. It won't be easy, now that she's pregnant with Creed's child, but having Rose taking care of her will be a tremendous help.

Rose is amazing! She's thirty years old, pale as porcelain, with stunning red lips, and a manner about her that makes her seem exactly what she claims to be.

An old soul.

Miranda met Rose four months ago at a karaoke bar and they hit it off immediately. It was as if Rose had known her all her life! After an hour of talking, she asked if Miranda could have any talent in the world, what would it be?

Miranda said, "This."

Rose said, "What do you mean?"

"I'd love to have a beautiful singing voice."

"And how would you use such a voice?" Rose said. "Would you want to be a famous singer?"

"Not really. I think I'd just like to sing for my husband."

"Do you have someone in mind?"

Miranda laughed. "Absolutely not!"

Rose shared the laugh, and the two new friends drank and enjoyed the singers for a time, and eventually Rose said, "You should try it."

"Try what?"

"You should get up on the stage and sing a song."

"Omigod! Miranda said. "I could never!"

"You can. Come on, I'll go with you."

"You'll sing with me?"

"If you wish."

Miranda looked at her new friend. For a minute, it almost seemed possible. But then she said, "No. Seriously, I could never get up and sing in front of total strangers."

"I understand," Rose said. She leaned over and whispered something in Miranda's ear that Miranda didn't quite catch.

Then she got up from the table, climbed on the stage, took the mike and said, "Ladies and gentlemen, I'd like to introduce you to a friend of mine. Her name is Miranda Rodriguez, and she's not going to sing a song for you tonight. I repeat, she is not going to sing for you. She's way too nervous. But she is going to take the first step. She's going to stand on the stage and face an audience for the first time in her life. Someday maybe Miranda will feel comfortable enough to sing for us, and that will be a special event, because she has a gorgeous voice. Trust me."

Rose pointed Miranda out to the crowd.

Miranda laughed and said, "Omigod!" and hid her face.

Rose said, "I know she'll come up on stage if you'll give her a big hand."

The crowd cheered and Rose chanted, "Miran-da! Miran-da!"

Miranda shook her head and stood up and climbed on the stage.

"For the love of God," she said, laughing.

Then one of Miranda's favorite songs began playing, and Rose handed her the mike and before she knew it, she was singing, and everyone in the place appeared to love it. Miranda knew she had a decent voice, but the reaction she was getting seemed insane!

It was the beginning of a friendship that grew into a strong bond between them. When Miranda wasn't busy studying or dating, she found herself singing in the karaoke bar and spending the night at Rose's loft on the upper east side.

One morning Rose said, "Have you given any thought to having children?"

Miranda laughed. "Absolutely not!"

Rose leaned over and whispered something into Miranda's ear, and a warmth came over her like she'd never experienced.

Rose has wanted a baby all her life but can't have children. Miranda has decided she wants to experience giving birth and feels she can find a use for the enormous sum of money Rose has offered to give her in exchange for Donovan Creed's baby.

As a result, three months ago Miranda stopped dating and got off the pill, and began drinking a special bark tea Rose brewed for her. And last week, right around the time Rose told her she was ready, low and behold, Creed called and asked her to meet him.

The terms of their contract stipulate Miranda will live with Rose during the entire pregnancy and for three months after the baby's birth, during which time Miranda will continue drinking the bark tea and breast feed the baby. Miranda agrees not to leave the house without Rose by her side, nor can she drink alcohol or have sex for the entire year. At the end of the year, the women will go their separate ways and Rose will take the baby.

Miranda signs the contract, and Rose hands her a certified check for ten million dollars.

"Aren't you concerned I'll tell Donovan about the baby someday?" Miranda asks.

"At the end of the year you may tell him anything you can remember," Rose says.

What an odd thing to say, Miranda thinks. She looks at the check. Ten million dollars for carrying a baby is an absurd amount of money.

Of course, Rose didn't start by offering ten million.

Her first offer was a quarter-million dollars.
But Miranda's always been a shrewd negotiator.   ·

PRISON
LIBRARY

Personal Message from John Locke:

I love writing books! But what I love even more is hearing from readers. If you enjoyed this or any of my other books, it would mean the world to me if you'd send a short email to introduce yourself and say hi. I always personally respond to my readers.

I would also love to put you on my mailing list to receive notifications about future books, updates, and contests.

Please visit my website, http://www.DonovanCreed.com, so I can personally thank you for trying my books.

John Locke

New York Times Best Selling Author

8th Member of the Kindle Million Sales Club
(which includes James Patterson, Stieg Larsson, George R.R. Martin and Lee Child, among others)

John Locke had 4 of the top 10 eBooks on Amazon/Kindle at the same time, including #1 and #2!

...Had 6 of the top 20, and 8 books in the top 43 at the same time!

...Has written 19 books in three years in four separate genres, all best-sellers!

...Has been published in numerous languages by many of the world's most prestigious publishing houses!

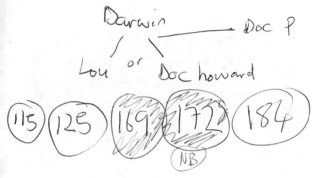

Darwin ——→ Doc P

Lou or Doc howard

(115) (125) (169) (172) (184)

NB

CPSIA information can be obtained at www.ICGtesting.com
Printed in the USA
LVOW07s1019251015

459650LV00018B/841/P

9 781937 698829